THOMAS MANN

DEATH IN VENICE

TRANSLATED BY
H. T. LOWE-PORTER

PENGUIN BOOKS

PENGUIN BOOKS

Published by the Penguin Group
Penguin Books Ltd, 27 Wrights Lane, London W8 5TZ, England
Penguin Books USA Inc., 375 Hudson Street, New York, New York 10014, USA
Penguin Books Australia Ltd, Ringwood, Victoria, Australia
Penguin Books Canada Ltd, 10 Alcorn Avenue, Toronto, Ontario, Canada M4V 3B2
Penguin Books (NZ) Ltd, 182–190 Wairau Road, Auckland 10, New Zealand

Penguin Books Ltd, Registered Offices: Harmondsworth, Middlesex, England

Der Tod in Venedig first published 1912
Death in Venice (with Tonia Kröger and Tristan)
first published by Martin Secker & Warburg Ltd 1928
Published in Penguin Books 1955
Death in Venice reprinted separately 1971
19 20 18

Printed in England by Clays Ltd, St Ives plc
Set in Monotype Bembo

DEATH IN VENICE

*

GUSTAVE ASCHENBACH – or von Aschenbach, as he had
been known officially since his fiftieth birthday – had set out
alone from his house in Prince Regent Street, Munich, for an
extended walk. It was a spring afternoon in that year of grace
19–, when Europe sat upon the anxious seat beneath a menace
that hung over its head for months. Aschenbach had sought
the open soon after tea. He was overwrought by a morning of
hard, nerve-taxing work, work which had not ceased to exact
his uttermost in the way of sustained concentration, conscien-
tiousness, and tact; and after the noon meal found himself
powerless to check the onward sweep of the productive mech-
anism within him, that *motus animi continuus* in which, accord-
ing to Cicero, eloquence resides. He had sought but not found
relaxation in sleep – though the wear and tear upon his system
had come to make a daily nap more and more imperative –
and now undertook a walk, in the hope that air and exercise
might send him back refreshed to a good evening's work.

May had begun, and after weeks of cold and wet a mock
summer had set in. The English Gardens, though in tenderest
leaf, felt as sultry as in August and were full of vehicles and
pedestrians near the city. But towards Aumeister the paths
were solitary and still, and Aschenbach strolled thither, stop-
ping awhile to watch the lively crowds in the restaurant
garden with its fringe of carriages and cabs. Thence he took
his homeward way outside the park and across the sunset
fields. By the time he reached the North Cemetery, however,
he felt tired, and a storm was brewing above Föhring; so he
waited at the stopping-place for a train to carry him back to
the city.

He found the neighbourhood quite empty. Not a wagon in sight, either on the paved Ungererstrasse, with its gleaming tram-lines stretching off towards Schwabing, nor on the Föhring highway. Nothing stirred behind the hedge in the stonemason's yard, where crosses, monuments, and commemorative tablets made a supernumerary and untenanted graveyard opposite the real one. The mortuary chapel, a structure in Byzantine style, stood facing it, silent in the gleam of the ebbing day. Its façade was adorned with Greek crosses and tinted hieratic designs, and displayed a symmetrically arranged selection of scriptural texts in gilded letters, all of them with a bearing upon the future life, such as: 'They are entering into the House of the Lord' and 'May the Light Everlasting shine upon them.' Aschenbach beguiled some minutes of his waiting with reading these formulas and letting his mind's eye lose itself in their mystical meaning. He was brought back to reality by the sight of a man standing in the portico, above the two apocalyptic beasts that guarded the staircase, and something not quite usual in this man's appearance gave his thoughts a fresh turn.

Whether he had come out of the hall through the bronze doors or mounted unnoticed from outside, it was impossible to tell. Aschenbach casually inclined to the first idea. He was of medium height, thin, beardless, and strikingly snub-nosed; he belonged to the red-haired type and possessed its milky, freckled skin. He was obviously not Bavarian; and the broad, straight-brimmed straw hat he had on even made him look distinctly exotic. True, he had the indigenous rucksack buckled on his back, wore a belted suit of yellowish woollen stuff, apparently frieze, and carried a grey mackintosh cape across his left forearm, which was propped against his waist. In his right hand, slantwise to the ground, he held an iron-shod stick, and braced himself against its crook, with his legs crossed. His chin was up, so that the Adam's apple looked very bald in the lean neck rising from the loose shirt: and he stood there sharply peering up into space out of colourless, red-lashed eyes, while two pronounced perpendicular furrows showed on his forehead in curious contrast to his little turned-up nose. Perhaps his heightened and heightening position helped out the impression Aschenbach received. At any rate, standing there as though at survey, the man had a bold and domineering, even a ruthless, air, and his lips completed the picture by seeming to curl back, either by reason of some deformity or else because he grimaced, being blinded by the sun in his face; they laid bare the long, white, glistening teeth to the gums.

Aschenbach's gaze, though unawares, had very likely been inquisitive and tactless; for he became suddenly conscious that the stranger was returning it, and indeed so directly, with such hostility, such plain intent to force the withdrawal of the other's eyes, that Aschenbach felt an unpleasant twinge, and turning his back, began to walk along the hedge, hastily resolving to give the man no further heed. He had forgotten him the next minute. Yet whether the pilgrim air the stranger wore kindled his fantasy or whether some other physical or psychical influence came in play, he could not tell; but he felt the most surprising consciousness of a widening of inward barriers, a kind of vaulting unrest, a youthfully ardent thirst for distant scenes – a feeling so lively and so new, or at least so long ago outgrown and forgot, that he stood there rooted to the spot, his eyes on the ground and his hands clasped behind him, exploring these sentiments of his, their bearing and scope.

True, what he felt was no more than a longing to travel; yet coming upon him with such suddenness and passion as to resemble a seizure, almost a hallucination. Desire projected itself visually: his fancy, not quite yet lulled since morning, imaged the marvels and terrors of the manifold earth. He saw. He beheld a landscape, a tropical marshland, beneath a reeking sky, steaming, monstrous, rank – a kind of primeval wilderness-world of islands, morasses, and alluvial channels. Hairy palm-trunks rose near and far out of lush brakes of fern, out of bottoms of crass vegetation, fat, swollen, thick with incredible bloom. There were trees, mis-shapen as a dream, that dropped their naked roots straight through the air into the ground or into water that was stagnant and shadowy and glassy-green, where mammoth milk-white blossoms floated, and strange high-shouldered birds with curious bills stood gazing sidewise without sound or stir. Among the knotted joints of a bamboo thicket the eyes of a crouching tiger gleamed – and he felt his heart throb with terror, yet with a longing inexplicable. Then the vision vanished. Aschenbach, shaking his head, took up his march once more along the hedge of the stonemason's yard.

He had, at least ever since he commanded means to get about the world at will, regarded travel as a necessary evil, to be endured now and again willy-nilly for the sake of one's health. Too busy with the tasks imposed upon him by his own ego and the European soul, too laden with the care and duty to create, too preoccupied to be an amateur of the gay outer world, he had been content to know as much of the earth's surface as he could without stirring far outside his own sphere – had, indeed, never even been tempted to leave Europe. Now more than ever, since his life was on the wane, since he could no longer brush aside as fanciful his artist fear of not having done, of not being finished before the works ran down, he had confined himself to close range, had hardly stepped outside the charming city which he had made his home and the rude country house he had built in the mountains, whither he went to spend the rainy summers.

And so the new impulse which thus late and suddenly swept over him was speedily made to conform to the pattern of self-discipline he had followed from his youth up. He had meant to bring his work, for which he lived, to a certain point before leaving for the country, and the thought of a leisurely ramble across the globe, which should take him away from his desk for months, was too fantastic and upsetting to be seriously entertained. Yet the source of the unexpected contagion was known to him only too well. This yearning for new and distant scenes, this craving for freedom, release, forgetfulness – they were he admitted to himself, an impulse towards flight, flight from the spot which was the daily theatre of a rigid, cold, and passionate service. That service he loved, had even almost come to love the enervating daily struggle between a proud, tenacious, well-tried will and this growing fatigue, which no one must suspect, nor the finished product betray by any faintest sign that his inspiration could ever flag or miss fire. On the other hand, it seemed the part of common sense not to span the bow too far, not to suppress summarily a need that so unequivocally asserted itself. He thought of his work, and the place where yesterday and again to-day he had been forced to lay it down, since it would not yield either to patient effort or a swift *coup de main*. Again and again he had tried to break or untie the knot – only to retire at last from the attack with a shiver of repugnance. Yet the difficulty was actually not a great one; what sapped his strength was distaste for the task, betrayed by a fastidiousness he could no longer satisfy. In his youth, indeed, the nature and inmost essence of the literary gift had been, to him, this very scrupulosity; for it had bridled and tempered his sensibilities, knowing full well that feeling is prone to be content with easy gains and blithe half-perfection. So now, perhaps, feeling, thus tyrannized, avenged itself by leaving him, refusing from now on to carry and wing his art and taking away with it all the ecstasy he had known in form and expression. Not that he was doing bad work. So much, at least, the years had brought him, that at any moment he might feel tranquilly assured of mastery. But he got no joy of it – not though a nation paid it homage. To him it seemed his work had ceased to be marked by that fiery play of fancy which is the product of joy, and more, and more potently, than any intrinsic content, forms in turn the joy of the receiving world. He dreaded the summer in the country, alone with the maid who prepared his food and the man who served him; dreaded to see the familiar mountain peaks and walls that would shut him up again with his heavy discontent. What he needed was a break, an interim existence, a means of passing time, other air and a new stock of blood, to make the summer tolerable and productive. Good, then, he would go a journey. Not far – not all the way to the tigers. A night in a *wagon-lit*, three or four weeks of lotus-eating at some one of the gay world's playgrounds in the lovely south. . . .

So ran his thoughts, while the clang of the electric tram drew nearer down the Ungererstrasse; and as he mounted the platform he decided to devote the evening to a study of maps and railway guides. Once in, he bethought him to look back after the man in the straw hat, the companion of this brief interval which had after all been so fruitful. But he was not in his former place, nor in the tram itself, nor yet at the next stop; in short, his whereabouts remained a mystery.

Gustave Aschenbach was born at L —, a country town in the province of Silesia. He was the son of an upper official in the judicature, and his forbears had all been officers, judges, departmental functionaries – men who lived their strict, decent, sparing lives in the service of king and state. Only once before had a livelier mentality – in the quality of a clergyman – turned up among them; but swifter, more perceptive blood had in the generation before the poet's flowed into the stock from the mother's side, she being the daughter of a Bohemian musical conductor. It was from her he had the foreign traits that betrayed themselves in his appearance. The union of dry, conscientious officialdom and ardent, obscure impulse, produced an artist – and this particular artist: author of the lucid and vigorous prose epic on the life of Frederick the Great; careful, tireless weaver of the richly patterned tapestry entitled *Maia*, a novel that gathers up the threads of many human destinies in the warp of a single idea; creator of that powerful narrative *The Abject*, which taught a whole grateful generation that a man can still be capable of moral resolution even after he has plumbed the depths of knowledge; and lastly – to complete the tale of works of his mature period – the writer of that impassioned discourse on the theme of Mind and Art whose ordered force and antithetic eloquence led serious critics to rank it with Schiller's *Simple and Sentimental Poetry*.

Aschenbach's whole soul, from the very beginning, was bent on fame – and thus, while not precisely precocious, yet thanks to the unmistakable trenchancy of his personal accent he was early ripe and ready for a career. Almost before he was out of high school he had a name. Ten years later he had learned to sit at his desk and sustain and live up to his growing reputation, to write gracious and pregnant phrases in letters that must needs be brief, for many claims press upon the solid and successful man. At forty, worn down by the strains and stresses of his actual task, he had to deal with a daily post heavy with tributes from his own and foreign countries.

Remote on one hand from the banal, on the other from the eccentric, his genius was calculated to win at once the adhesion of the general public and the admiration, both sympathetic and stimulating, of the connoisseur. From childhood up he was pushed on every side to achievement, and achievement of no ordinary kind; and so his young days never knew the sweet idleness and blithe *laissez aller* that belong to youth. A nice observer once said of him in company – it was at the time when he fell ill in Vienna in his thirty-fifth year: 'You see, Aschenbach has always lived like this' – here the speaker closed the fingers of his left hand to a fist – 'never like this' – and he let his open hand hang relaxed from the back of his chair. It was apt. And this attitude was the more morally valiant in that Aschenbach was not by nature robust – he was only called to the constant tension of his career, not actually born to it.

By medical advice he had been kept from school and educated at home. He had grown up solitary, without comradeship;

yet had early been driven to see that he belonged to those whose talent is not so much out of the common as is the physical basis on which talent relies for its fulfilment. It is a seed that gives early of its fruit, whose powers seldom reach a ripe old age. But his favourite motto was 'Hold fast'; indeed, in his novel on the life of Frederick the Great he envisaged nothing else than the apotheosis of the old hero's word of command, '*Durchhalten*,' which seemed to him the epitome of fortitude under suffering. Besides, he deeply desired to live to a good old age, for it was his conviction that only the artist to whom it has been granted to be fruitful on all stages of our human scene can be truly great, or universal, or worthy of honour.

Bearing the burden of his genius, then, upon such slender shoulders and resolved to go so far, he had the more need of discipline – and discipline, fortunately, was his native inheritance from the father's side. At forty, at fifty, he was still living as he had commenced to live in the years when others are prone to waste and revel, dream high thoughts and postpone fulfilment. He began his day with a cold shower over chest and back; then, setting a pair of tall wax candles in silver holders at the head of his manuscript, he sacrificed to art, in two or three hours of almost religious fervour, the powers he had assembled in sleep. Outsiders might be pardoned for believing that his *Maia* world and the epic amplitude revealed by the life of Frederick were a manifestation of great power working under high pressure, that they came forth, as it were, all in one breath. It was the more triumph for his morale; for the truth was that they were heaped up to greatness in layer after layer, in long days of work, out of hundreds and hundreds of single inspirations; they owed their excellence, both of mass and detail, to one thing and one alone: that their creator could hold out for years under the strain of the same piece of work, with an endurance and a tenacity of purpose like that which had conquered his native province of Silesia, devoting to actual composition none but his best and freshest hours.

For an intellectual product of any value to exert an immediate influence which shall also be deep and lasting, it must rest
on an inner harmony, yes, an affinity, between the personal
destiny of its author and that of his contemporaries in general.
Men do not know why they award fame to one work of art
rather than another. Without being in the faintest connois-
seurs, they think to justify the warmth of their commendations
by discovering in it a hundred virtues, whereas the real ground
of their applause is inexplicable – it is sympathy. Aschenbach
had once given direct expression – though in an unobtrusive
place – to the idea that almost everything conspicuously great
is great in despite: has come into being in defiance of affliction
and pain, poverty, destitution, bodily weakness, vice, passion,
and a thousand other obstructions. And that was more than
observation – it was the fruit of experience, it was precisely
the formula of his life and fame, it was the key to his work.
What wonder, then, if it was also the fixed character, the outward gesture, of his most individual figures?

The new type of hero favoured by Aschenbach, and recurring many times in his works, had early been analysed by a
shrewd critic: 'The conception of an intellectual and virginal
manliness, which clenches its teeth and stands in modest defiance of the swords and spears that pierce its side.' That was
beautiful, it was *spirituel*, it was exact, despite the suggestion
of too great passivity it held. Forbearance in the face of fate,
beauty constant under torture, are not merely passive. They
are a positive achievement, an explicit triumph; and the figure
of Sebastian is the most beautiful symbol, if not of art as a
whole, yet certainly of the art we speak of here. Within that
world of Aschenbach's creation were exhibited many phases
of this theme: there was the aristocratic self-command that is
eaten out within and for as long as it can conceals its biologic
decline from the eyes of the world; the sere and ugly outside,
hiding the embers of smouldering fire – and having power to
fan them to so pure a flame as to challenge supremacy in the

domain of beauty itself; the pallid languors of the flesh, contrasted with the fiery ardours of the spirit within, which can fling a whole proud people down at the foot of the Cross, at the feet of its own sheer self-abnegation; the gracious bearing preserved in the stern, stark service of form; the unreal, precarious existence of the born intrigant with its swiftly enervating alternation of schemes and desires – all these human fates and many more of their like one read in Aschenbach's pages, and reading them might doubt the existence of any other kind of heroism than the heroism born of weakness. And, after all, what kind could be truer to the spirit of the times? Gustave Aschenbach was the poet-spokesman of all those who labour at the edge of exhaustion; of the overburdened, of those who are already worn out but still hold themselves upright; of all our modern moralizers of accomplishment, with stunted growth and scanty resources, who yet contrive by skilful husbanding and prodigious spasms of will to produce, at least for a while, the effect of greatness. There are many such, they are the heroes of the age. And in Aschenbach's pages they saw themselves; he justified, he exalted them, he sang their praise – and they, they were grateful, they heralded his fame.

He had been young and crude with the times and by them badly counselled. He had taken false steps, blundered, exposed himself, offended in speech and writing against tact and good sense. But he had attained to honour, and honour, he used to say, is the natural goal towards which every considerable talent presses with whip and spur. Yes, one might put it that his whole career had been one conscious and overweening ascent to honour, which left in the rear all the misgivings or self-derogation which might have hampered him.

What pleases the public is lively and vivid delineation which makes no demands on the intellect; but passionate and absolutist youth can only be enthralled by a problem. And Aschenbach was as absolute, as problematist, as any youth of them all. He had done homage to intellect, had overworked the soil of knowledge and ground up her seed-corn; had turned his back on the 'mysteries', called genius itself in question, held up art to scorn – yes, even while his faithful following revelled in the characters he created, he, the young artist, was taking away the breath of the twenty-year-olds with his cynic utterances on the nature of art and the artist life.

But it seems that a noble and active mind blunts itself against nothing so quickly as the sharp and bitter irritant of know-ledge. And certain it is that the youth's constancy of purpose, no matter how painfully conscientious, was shallow beside the mature resolution of the master of his craft, who made a right-about-face, turned his back on the realm of knowledge, and passed it by with averted face, lest it lame his will or power of action, paralyse his feelings or his passions, deprive any of these of their conviction or utility. How else interpret the oft-cited story of *The Abject* than as a rebuke to the excesses of a psychology-ridden age, embodied in the delineation of the weak and silly fool who manages to lead fate by the nose; driving his wife, out of sheer innate pusillanimity, into the arms of a beardless youth, and making this disaster an excuse for trifling away the rest of his life?

With rage the author here rejects the rejected, casts out the outcast – and the measure of his fury is the measure of his con-demnation of all moral shilly-shallying. Explicitly he re-nounces sympathy with the abyss, explicitly he refutes the flabby humanitarianism of the phrase: '*Tout comprendre c'est tout pardonner.*' What was here unfolding, or rather was already in full bloom, was the 'miracle of regained detachment', which a little later became the theme of one of the author's dialogues, dwelt upon not without a certain oracular emphasis. Strange sequence of thought! Was it perhaps an intellectual consequence of this rebirth, this new austerity, that from now on his style showed an almost exaggerated sense of beauty, a lofty purity, symmetry, and simplicity, which gave his productions a stamp of the classic, of conscious and deliberate mastery? And yet: this moral fibre, surviving the hampering and disintegrating effect of knowledge, does it not result in its turn in a dangerous simplification, in a tendency to equate the world and the human soul, and thus to strengthen the hold of the evil, the forbidden, and the ethically impossible? And has not form two aspects? Is it not moral and immoral at once; moral in so far as it is the expression and result of discipline, immoral – yes, actually hostile to morality – in that of its very essence it is indifferent to good and evil, and deliberately concerned to make the moral world stoop beneath its proud and undivided sceptre?

Be that as it may. Development is destiny; and why should a career attended by applause and adulation of the masses necessarily take the same course as one which does not share the glamour and the obligations of fame? Only the incorrigible bohemian smiles or scoffs when a man of transcendent gifts outgrows his carefree prentice stage, recognizes his own worth and forces the world to recognize it too and pay it homage, though he puts on a courtly bearing to hide his bitter struggles and his loneliness. Again, the play of a developing talent must give its possessor joy, if of a wilful, defiant kind. With time, an official note, something almost expository, crept into Gustave Aschenbach's method. His later style gave up the old sheer audacities, the fresh and subtle nuances – it became fixed and exemplary, conservative, formal, even formulated. Like Louis XIV – or as tradition has it of him – Aschenbach, as he went on in years, banished from his style every common word. It was at this time that the school authorities adopted selections from his works into their text-books. And he found it only fitting – and had not thought but to accept – when a German prince signalized his accession to the throne by conferring upon the poet-author of the life of Frederick the Great on his fiftieth birthday the letters-patent of nobility.

He had roved about for a few years, trying this place and

that as a place of residence, before choosing, as he soon did, the city of Munich for his permanent home. And there he lived, enjoying among his fellow-citizens the honour which is in rare cases the reward of intellectual eminence. He married young, the daughter of a university family; but after a brief term of wedded happiness his wife had died. A daughter, already married, remained to him. A son he never had.

Gustave von Aschenbach was somewhat below middle height, dark and smooth-shaven, with a head that looked rather too large for his almost delicate figure. He wore his hair brushed back; it was thin at the parting, bushy and grey on the temples, framing a lofty, rugged, knotty brow – if one may so characterize it. The nose-piece of his rimless gold spectacles cut into the base of his thick, aristocratically hooked nose. The mouth was large, often lax, often suddenly narrow and tense; the cheeks lean and furrowed, the pronounced chin slightly cleft. The vicissitudes of fate, it seemed, must have passed over his head, for he held it, plaintively, rather on one side; yet it was art, not the stern discipline of an active career, that had taken over the office of modelling these features. Behind this brow were born the flashing thrust and parry of the dialogue between Frederick and Voltaire on the theme of war; these eyes, weary and sunken, gazing through their glasses, had beheld the blood-stained inferno of the hospitals in the Seven Years' War. Yes, personally speaking too, art heightens life. She gives deeper joy, she consumes more swiftly. She engraves adventures of the spirit and the mind in the faces of her votaries; let them lead outwardly a life of the most cloistered calm, she will in the end produce in them a fastidiousness, an over-refinement, a nervous fever and exhaustion, such as a career of extravagant passions and pleasures can hardly show.

Eager though he was to be off, Aschenbach was kept in Munich by affairs both literary and practical for some two weeks after that walk of his. But at length he ordered his country home

put ready against his return within the next few weeks, and on
a day between the middle and the end of May took the evening
train for Trieste, where he stopped only twenty-four hours,
embarking for Pola the next morning but one.

What he sought was a fresh scene, without associations,
which should yet be not too out-of-the-way; and accordingly
he chose an island in the Adriatic, not far off the Istrian coast.
It had been well known some years, for its splendidly rugged
cliff formations on the side next the open sea, and its population, clad in a bright flutter of rags and speaking an outlandish
tongue. But there was rain and heavy air; the society at the
hotel was provincial Austrian, and limited; besides, it annoyed
him not to be able to get at the sea – he missed the close and
soothing contact which only a gentle sandy slope affords. He
could not feel this was the place he sought; an inner impulse
made him wretched, urging him on he knew not whither; he
racked his brains, he looked up boats, then all at once his goal
stood plain before his eyes. But of course! When one wanted
to arrive overnight at the incomparable, the fabulous, the like-
nothing-else-in-the-world, where was it one went? Why, obviously; he had intended to go there, what ever was he doing
here? A blunder. He made all haste to correct it, announcing
his departure at once. Ten days after his arrival on the island
a swift motor-boat bore him and his luggage in the misty
dawning back across the water to the naval station, where he
landed only to pass over the landing-stage and on to the wet
decks of a ship lying there with steam up for the passage to
Venice.

It was an ancient hulk belonging to an Italian line, obsolete,
dingy, grimed with soot. A dirty hunchbacked sailor, smirk-
ingly polite, conducted him at once belowships to a cavern-
ous, lamplit cabin. There behind a table sat a man with a beard
like a goat's; he had his hat on the back of his head, a cigar-
stump in the corner of his mouth; he reminded Aschenbach of
an old-fashioned circus-director. This person put the usual

questions and wrote out a ticket to Venice, which he issued to
the traveller with many commercial flourishes.

'A ticket for Venice,' he repeated, stretching out his arm to
dip the pen into the thick ink in a tilted ink-stand. 'One first-
class to Venice! Here you are, *signore mio*.' He made some
scrawls on the paper, strewed bluish sand on it out of a box,
thereafter letting the sand run off into an earthen vessel, folded
the paper with bony yellow fingers, and wrote on the outside.
'An excellent choice,' he rattled on. 'Ah, Venice! What a
glorious city! Irresistibly attractive to the cultured man for her
past history as well as her present charm.' His copious gesturings and empty phrases gave the odd impression that he feared
the traveller might alter his mind. He changed Aschenbach's
note, laying the money on the spotted table-cover with the
glibness of a croupier. 'A pleasant visit to you, signore,' he
said, with a melodramatic bow. 'Delighted to serve you.'
Then he beckoned and called out: 'Next' as though a stream
of passengers stood waiting to be served, though in point of
fact there was not one. Aschenbach returned to the upper deck.

He leaned an arm on the railing and looked at the idlers
lounging along the quay to watch the boat go out. Then he
turned his attention to his fellow-passengers. Those of the
second class, both men and women, were squatted on their
bundles of luggage on the forward deck. The first cabin consisted of a group of lively youths, clerks from Pola, evidently,
who had made up a pleasure excursion to Italy and were not
a little thrilled at the prospect, bustling about and laughing
with satisfaction at the stir they made. They leaned over the
railings and shouted, with a glib command of epithet, derisory
remarks at such of their fellow-clerks as they saw going to
business along the quay; and these in turn shook their sticks
and shouted as good back again. One of the party, in a dandi-
fied buff suit, a rakish panama with a coloured scarf, and a red
cravat, was loudest of the loud: he outcrowed all the rest.
Aschenbach's eye dwelt on him, and he was shocked to see

that the apparent youth was no youth at all. He was an old
man, beyond a doubt, with wrinkles and crow's-feet round
eyes and mouth; the dull carmine of the cheeks was rouge, the
brown hair a wig. His neck was shrunken and sinewy, his
turned-up moustaches and small imperial were dyed, and the
unbroken double row of yellow teeth he showed when he
laughed were but too obviously a cheapish false set. He wore
a seal ring on each forefinger, but the hands were those of an
old man. Aschenbach was moved to shudder as he watched
the creature and his association with the rest of the group.
Could they not see he was old, that he had no right to wear
the clothes they wore or pretend to be one of them? But they
were used to him, it seemed; they suffered him among them,
they paid back his jokes in kind and the playful pokes in the
ribs he gave them. How could they? Aschenbach put his hand
to his brow, he covered his eyes, for he had slept little, and
they smarted. He felt not quite canny, as though the world
were suffering a dreamlike distortion of perspective which he
might arrest by shutting it all out for a few minutes and then
looking at it afresh. But instead he felt a floating sensation, and
opened his eyes with unreasoning alarm to find that the ship's
dark sluggish bulk was slowly leaving the jetty. Inch by inch,
with the to-and-fro motion of her machinery, the strip of
iridescent dirty water widened, the boat manoeuvred clumsily
and turned her bow to the open sea. Aschenbach moved over
to the starboard side, where the hunchbacked sailor had set up
a deck-chair for him, and a steward in a greasy dress-coat asked
for orders.

The sky was grey, the wind humid. Harbour and island
dropped behind, all sight of land soon vanished in mist. Flakes
of sodden, clammy soot fell upon the still undried deck. Before the boat was an hour out a canvas had to be spread as a
shelter from the rain.

Wrapped in his cloak, a book in his lap, our traveller rested;
the hours slipped by unawares. It stopped raining, the canvas

was taken down. The horizon was visible right round: beneath the sombre dome of the sky stretched the vast plain of empty sea. But immeasurable unarticulated space weakens our power to measure time as well: the time-sense falters and grows dim. Strange, shadowy figures passed and repassed – the elderly coxcomb, the goat-bearded man from the bowels of the ship – with vague gesturings and mutterings through the traveller's mind as he lay. He fell asleep.

At midday he was summoned to luncheon in a corridor-like saloon with the sleeping-cabins giving off it. He ate at the head of the long table; the party of clerks, including the old man, sat with the jolly captain at the other end, where they had been carousing since ten o'clock. The meal was wretched, and soon done. Aschenbach was driven to seek the open and look at the sky – perhaps it would lighten presently above Venice.

He had not dreamed it could be otherwise, for the city had ever given him a brilliant welcome. But sky and sea remained leaden, with spurts of fine, mistlike rain; he reconciled himself to the idea of seeing a different Venice from that he had always approached on the landward side. He stood by the foremast, his gaze on the distance, alert for the first glimpse of the coast. And he thought of the melancholy and susceptible poet who had once seen the towers and turrets of his dreams rise out of these waves; repeated the rhythms born of his awe, his mingled emotions of joy and suffering – and easily susceptible to a pre-science already shaped with him, he asked his own sober, weary heart if a new enthusiasm, a new preoccupation, some late adventure of the feelings could still be in store for the idle traveller.

The flat coast showed on the right, the sea was soon populous with fishing-boats. The Lido appeared and was left behind as the ship glided at half speed through the narrow harbour of the same name, coming to a full stop on the lagoon in sight of garish, badly built houses. Here it waited for the boat bringing the sanitary inspector.

An hour passed. One had arrived – and yet not. There was no conceivable haste – yet one felt harried. The youths from Pola were on deck, drawn hither by the martial sound of horns coming across the water from the direction of the Public Gardens. They had drunk a good deal of Asti and were moved to shout and hurrah at the drilling *bersaglieri*. But the young-old man was a truly repulsive sight in the condition to which his company with youth had brought him. He could nòt carry his wine like them: he was pitiably drunk. He swayed as he stood – watery-eyed, a cigarette between his shaking fingers, keeping upright with difficulty. He could not have taken a step without falling and knew better than to stir, but his spirits were deplorably high. He buttonholed anyone who came within reach, he stuttered, he giggled, he leered, he fatuously shook his beringed old forefinger; his tongue kept seeking the corner of his mouth in a suggestive motion ugly to behold. Aschenbach's brow darkened as he looked, and there came over him once more a dazed sense, as though things about him were just slightly losing their ordinary perspective, beginning to show a distortion that might merge into the grotesque. He was prevented from dwelling on the feeling, for now the machinery began to thud again, and the ship took up its passage through the Canal di San Marco which had been interrupted so near the goal.

He saw it once more, that landing-place that takes the breath away, that amazing group of incredible structures the Republic set up to meet the awe-struck eye of the approaching seafarer: the airy splendour of the palace and Bridge of Sighs, the columns of lion and saint on the shore, the glory of the projecting flank of the fairy temple, the vista of gateway and clock. Looking, he thought that to come to Venice by the station is like entering a palace by the back door. No one should approach, save by the high seas as he was doing now, this most improbable of cities.

The engines stopped. Gondolas pressed alongside, the land-

ing-stairs were let down, customs officials came on board and
did their office, people began to go ashore. Aschenbach ordered a gondola. He meant to take up his abode by the sea
and needed to be conveyed with his luggage to the landing-
stage of the little steamers that ply between the city and the
Lido. They called down his order to thè surface of the water
where the gondoliers were quarrelling in dialect. Then came
another delay while his trunk was worried down the ladder-
like stairs. Thus he was forced to endure the importunities
of the ghastly young-old man, whose drunken state obscurely
urged him to pay the stranger the honour of a formal farewell. 'We wish you a very pleasant sojourn,' he babbled, bowing and scraping. 'Pray keep us in mind. *Au revoir, excusez et
bon jour, votre Excellence.*' He drooled, he blinked, he licked the
corner of his mouth, the little imperial bristled on his elderly
chin. He put the tips of two fingers to his mouth and said
thickly: 'Give her our love, will you, the p–pretty little dear'
– here his upper plate came away and fell down on the lower
one. . . . Aschenbach escaped. 'Little sweety-sweety-sweet-
heart' he heard behind him, gurgled and stuttered, as he
climbed down the rope stair into the boat.

Is there anyone but must repress a secret thrill, on arriving
in Venice for the first time – or returning thither after long
absence – and stepping into a Venetian gondola? That singular conveyance, come down unchanged from ballad times,
black as nothing else on earth except a coffin – what pictures
it calls up of lawless, silent adventures in the plashing night;
or even more, what visions of death itself, the bier and solemn
rites and last soundless voyage! And has anyone remarked that
the seat in such a bark, the arm-chair lacquered in coffin-black,
and dully black-upholstered, is the softest, most luxurious,
most relaxing seat in the world? Aschenbach realized it when
he had let himself down at the gondolier's feet, opposite his
luggage, which lay neatly composed on the vessel's beak. The
rowers still gestured fiercely; he heard their harsh, incoherent

tones. But the strange stillness of the water-city seemed to take
up their voices gently, to disembody and scatter them over the
sea. It was warm here in the harbour. The lukewarm air of the
sirocco breathed upon him, he leaned back among his cushions
and gave himself to the yielding element, closing his eyes for
very pleasure in an indolence as unaccustomed as sweet. 'The
trip will be short,' he thought, and wished it might last forever. They gently swayed away from the boat with its bustle
and clamour of voices.

It grew still and stiller all about. No sound but the splash of
the oars, the hollow slap of the wave against the steep, black,
halbert-shaped beak of the vessel, and one sound more – a
muttering by fits and starts, expressed as it were by the motion
of his arms, from the lips of the gondolier. He was talking to
himself, between his teeth. Aschenbach glanced up and saw
with surprise that the lagoon was widening, his vessel was
headed for the open sea. Evidently it would not do to give
himself up to sweet *far niente*; he must see his wishes carried
out.

'You are to take me to the steamboat landing, you know,'
he said, half turning round towards it. The muttering stopped.
There was no reply.

'Take me to the steamboat landing,' he repeated, and this
time turned quite round and looked up into the face of the
gondolier as he stood there on his little elevated deck, high
against the pale grey sky. The man had an unpleasing, even
brutish face, and wore blue clothes like a sailor's, with a yellow
sash; a shapeless straw hat with the braid torn at the brim
perched rakishly on his head. His facial structure, as well as the
curling blond moustache under the short snub nose, showed
him to be of non-Italian stock. Physically rather undersized, so
that one would not have expected him to be very muscular,
he pulled vigorously at the oar, putting all his body-weight
behind each stroke. Now and then the effort he made curled
back his lips and bared his white teeth to the gums. He spoke

in a decided, almost curt voice, looking out to sea over his fare's head: 'The signore is going to the Lido.'

Aschenbach answered: 'Yes, I am. But I only took the gondola to cross over to San Marco. I am using the *vaporetto* from there.'

'But the signore cannot use the *vaporetto*.'

'And why not?'

'Because the *vaporetto* does not take luggage.'

It was true. Aschenbach remembered it. He made no answer. But the man's gruff, overbearing manner, so unlike the usual courtesy of his countrymen towards the stranger, was intolerable. Aschenbach spoke again: 'That is my own affair. I may want to give my luggage in deposit. You will turn round.'

No answer. The oar splashed, the wave struck dull against the prow. And the muttering began anew, the gondolier talked to himself, between his teeth.

What should the traveller do? Alone on the water with this tongue-tied, obstinate, uncanny man, he saw no way of enforcing his will. And if only he did not excite himself, how pleasantly he might rest! Had he not wished the voyage might last forever? The wisest thing – and how much the pleasantest! – was to let matters take their own course. A spell of indolence was upon him; it came from the chair he sat in – this low, black-upholstered arm-chair, so gently rocked at the hands of the despotic boatman in his rear. The thought passed dreamily through Aschenbach's brain that perhaps he had fallen into the clutches of a criminal; it had not power to rouse him to action. More annoying was the simpler explanation: that the man was only trying to extort money. A sense of duty, a recollection, as it were, that this ought to be prevented, made him collect himself to say:

'How much do you ask for the trip?'

And the gondolier, gazing out over his head, replied: 'The signore will pay.'

There was an established reply to this; Aschenbach made it, mechanically:

'I will pay nothing whatever if you do not take me where I want to go.'

'The signore wants to go to the Lido.'

'But not with you.'

'I am a good rower, signore, I will row you well.'

'So much is true,' thought Aschenbach, and again he relaxed. 'That is true, you row me well. Even if you mean to rob me, even if you hit me in the back with your oar and send me down to the kingdom of Hades, even then you will have rowed me well.'

But nothing of the sort happened. Instead, they fell in with company: a boat came alongside and waylaid them, full of men and women singing to guitar and mandolin. They rowed persistently bow for bow with the gondola and filled the silence that had rested on the waters with their lyric love of gain. Aschenbach tossed money into the hat they held out. The music stopped at once, they rowed away. And once more the gondolier's mutter became audible as he talked to himself in fits and snatches.

Thus they rowed on, rocked by the wash of a steamer returning citywards. At the landing two municipal officials were walking up and down with their hands behind their backs and their faces turned towards the lagoon. Aschenbach was helped on shore by the old man with a boat-hook who is the permanent feature of every landing-stage in Venice; and having no small change to pay the boatman, crossed over into the hotel opposite. His wants were supplied in the lobby, but when he came back his possessions were already on a hand-car on the quay, and gondola and gondolier were gone.

'He ran away, signore,' said the old boatman. 'A bad lot, a man without a licence. He is the only gondolier without one. The others telephoned over, and he knew we were on the look-out, so he made off.'

Aschenbach shrugged.

'The signore has had a ride for nothing,' said the old man, and held out his hat. Aschenbach dropped some coins. He directed that his luggage be taken to the Hôtel des Bains and followed the hand-car through the avenue, that white-blossoming avenue with taverns, booths, and pensions on either side it, which runs across the island diagonally to the beach.

He entered the hotel from the garden terrace at the back and passed through the vestibule and hall into the office. His arrival was expected, and he was served with courtesy and dispatch. The manager, a small, soft, dapper man with a black moustache and a caressing way with him, wearing a French frock-coat, himself took him up in the lift and showed him his room. It was a pleasant chamber, furnished in cherry-wood, with lofty windows looking out to sea. It was decorated with strong-scented flowers. Aschenbach, as soon as he was alone, and while they brought in his trunk and bags and disposed them in the room, went up to one of the windows and stood looking out upon the beach in its afternoon emptiness, and at the sunless sea, now full and sending long, low waves with rhythmic beat upon the sand.

A solitary, unused to speaking of what he sees and feels, has mental experiences which are at once more intense and less articulate than those of a gregarious man. They are sluggish, yet more wayward, and never without a melancholy tinge. Sights and impressions which others brush aside with a glance, a light comment, a smile, occupy him more than their due; they sink silently in, they take on meaning, they become experience, emotion, adventure. Solitude gives birth to the original in us, to beauty unfamiliar and perilous – to poetry. But also, it gives birth to the opposite: to the perverse, the illicit, the absurd. Thus the traveller's mind still dwelt with disquiet on the episodes of his journey hither: on the horrible old fop with his drivel about a mistress, on the outlaw boatman and his lost tip. They did not offend his reason, they

hardly afforded food for thought; yet they seemed by their
very nature fundamentally strange, and thereby vaguely dis-
quieting. Yet here was the sea; even in the midst of such
thoughts he saluted it with his eyes, exulting that Venice was
near and accessible. At length he turned round, disposed his
personal belongings and made certain arrangements with the
chambermaid for his comfort, washed, and was conveyed to
the ground floor by the green-uniformed Swiss who ran the
lift.

He took tea on the terrace facing the sea and afterwards
went down and walked some distance along the shore prom-
enade in the direction of Hôtel Excelsior. When he came back
it seemed to be time to change for dinner. He did so, slowly
and methodically as his way was, for he was accustomed to
work while he dressed; but even so he found himself a little
early when he entered the hall, where a large number of
guests had collected – strangers to each other and affecting
mutual indifference, yet united in expectancy of the meal.
He picked up a paper, sat down in a leather arm-chair, and
took stock of the company, which compared most favourably
with that he had just left.

This was a broad and tolerant atmosphere, of wide horizons.
Subdued voices were speaking most of the principal European
tongues. That uniform of civilization, the conventional evening dress, gave outward conformity to the varied types. There
were long, dry Americans, large-familied Russians, English
ladies, German children with French *bonnes*. The Slavic element predominated, it seemed. In Aschenbach's neighbourhood Polish was being spoken.

Round a wicker table next him was gathered a group of
young folk in charge of a governess or companion – three
young girls, perhaps fifteen to seventeen years old, and a long-
haired boy of about fourteen. Aschenbach noticed with aston-
ishment the lad's perfect beauty. His face recalled the noblest
moment of Greek sculpture – pale, with a sweet reserve, with

clustering honey-coloured ringlets, the brow and nose descending in one line, the winning mouth, the expression of pure and godlike serenity. Yet with all this chaste perfection of form it was of such unique personal charm that the observer thought he had never seen, either in nature or art, anything so utterly happy and consummate. What struck him further was the strange contrast the group afforded, a difference in educational method, so to speak, shown in the way the brother and sisters were clothed and treated. The girls, the eldest of whom was practically grown up, were dressed with an almost disfiguring austerity. All three wore half-length slate-coloured frocks of cloister-like plainness, arbitrarily unbecoming in cut, with white turn-over collars as their only adornment. Every grace of outline was wilfully suppressed; their hair lay smoothly plastered to their heads, giving them a vacant expression, like a nun's. All this could only be by the mother's orders; but there was no trace of the same pedagogic severity in the case of the boy. Tenderness and softness, it was plain, conditioned his existence. No scissors had been put to the lovely hair that (like the Spinnario's) curled about his brows, above his ears, longer still in the neck. He wore an English sailor suit, with quilted sleeves that narrowed round the delicate wrists of his long and slender though still childish hands. And this suit, with its breast-knot, lacings, and embroideries, lent the slight figure something 'rich and strange', a spoilt, exquisite air. The observer saw him in half profile, with one foot in its black patent leather advanced, one elbow resting on the arm of his basket-chair, the cheek nestled into the closed hand in a pose of easy grace, quite unlike the stiff subservient mien which was evidently habitual to his sisters. Was he delicate? His facial tint was ivory-white against the golden darkness of his clustering locks. Or was he simply a pampered darling, the object of a self-willed and partial love? Aschenbach inclined to think the latter. For in almost every artist nature is inborn a wanton and treacherous proneness to side with the beauty that breaks hearts, to single out aristocratic pretensions and pay them homage.

A waiter announced, in English, that dinner was served. Gradually the company dispersed through the glass doors into the dining-room. Late-comers entered from the vestibule or the lifts. Inside, dinner was being served; but the young Poles still sat and waited about their wicker table. Aschenbach felt comfortable in his deep arm-chair, he enjoyed the beauty before his eyes, he waited with them.

The governess, a short, stout, red-faced person, at length gave the signal. With lifted brows she pushed back her chair and made a bow to the tall woman, dressed in palest grey, who now entered the hall. This lady's abundant jewels were pearls, her manner was cool and measured; the fashion of her gown and the arrangement of her lightly powdered hair had the simplicity prescribed in certain circles whose piety and aristocracy are equally marked. She might have been, in Germany, the wife of some high official. But there was something faintly fabulous, after all, in her appearance, though lent it solely by the pearls she wore: they were well-nigh priceless, and consisted of ear-rings and a three-stranded necklace, very long, with gems the size of cherries.

The brother and sisters had risen briskly. They bowed over their mother's hand to kiss it, she turning away from them, with a slight smile on her face, which was carefully preserved but rather sharp-nosed and worn. She addressed a few words in French to the governess, then moved towards the glass door. The children followed, the girls in order of age, then the governess, and last the boy. He chanced to turn before he crossed the threshold, and as there was no one else in the room, his strange, twilit grey eyes met Aschenbach's, as our traveller sat there with the paper on his knee, absorbed in looking after the group.

There was nothing singular, of course, in what he had seen. They had not gone in to dinner before their mother, they had waited, given her a respectful salute, and but observed the right and proper forms on entering the room. Yet they had done all this so expressly, with such self-respecting dignity, discipline, and sense of duty that Aschenbach was impressed. He lingered still a few minutes, then he, too, went into the dining-room, where he was shown to a table far off from the Polish family, as he noted at once, with a stirring of regret.

Tired, yet mentally alert, he beguiled the long, tedious meal with abstract, even with transcendent matters: pondered the mysterious harmony that must come to subsist between the individual human being and the universal law, in order that human beauty may result; passed on to general problems of form and art, and came at length to the conclusion that what seemed to him fresh and happy thoughts were like the flattering inventions of a dream, which the waking sense proves worthless and insubstantial. He spent the evening in the park, that was sweet with the odours of evening – sitting, smoking, wandering about; went to bed betimes, and passed the night in deep, unbroken sleep, visited, however, by varied and lively dreams.

The weather next day was no more promising. A land breeze blew. Beneath a colourless, overcast sky the sea lay sluggish, and as it were shrunken, so far withdrawn as to leave bare several rows of long sand-banks. The horizon looked close and prosaic. When Aschenbach opened his window he thought he smelt the stagnant odour of the lagoons.

He felt suddenly out of sorts and already began to think of leaving. Once, years before, after weeks of bright spring weather, this wind had found him out; it had been so bad as to force him to flee from the city like a fugitive. And now it seemed beginning again – the same feverish distaste, the pressure on his temples, the heavy eyelids. It would be a nuisance to change again; but if the wind did not turn, this was no place for him. To be on the safe side, he did not entirely unpack. At nine o'clock he went down to the buffet, which lay between the hall and the dining-room and served as breakfast-room.

A solemn stillness reigned here, such as it is the ambition of all large hotels to achieve. The waiters moved on noiseless feet. A rattling of tea-things, a whispered word – and no other sounds. In a corner diagonally to the door, two tables off his own, Aschenbach saw the Polish girls with their governess. They sat there very straight, in their stiff blue linen frocks with little turn-over collars and cuffs, their ash-blond hair newly brushed flat, their eyelids red from sleep, and handed each other the marmalade. They had nearly finished their meal. The boy was not there.

Aschenbach smiled. 'Aha, little Phaeax,' he thought. 'It seems you are privileged to sleep yourself out.' With sudden gaiety he quoted:

'*Oft veränderten Schmuck und warme Bäder und Ruhe.*'

He took a leisurely breakfast. The porter came up with his braided cap in his hand, to deliver some letters that had been sent on. Aschenbach lighted a cigarette and opened a few letters and thus was still seated to witness the arrival of the sluggard.

He entered through the glass doors and walked diagonally across the room to his sisters at their table. He walked with extraordinary grace – the carriage of the body, the action of the knee, the way he set down his foot in its white shoe – it was all so light, it was at once dainty and proud, it wore an added charm in the childish shyness which made him twice turn his head as he crossed the room, made him give a quick glance and then drop his eyes. He took his seat, with a smile and a murmured word in his soft and blurry tongue; and Aschenbach, sitting so that he could see him in profile, was astonished anew, yes, startled, at the godlike beauty of the human being. The lad had on a light sailor suit of blue and white striped cotton, with a red silk breast-knot and a simple white standing collar round the neck – a not very elegant effect – yet above this collar the head was poised like a flower,

in incomparable loveliness. It was the head of Eros, with the
yellowish bloom of Parian marble, with fine serious brows,
and dusky clustering ringlets standing out in soft plenteous-
ness over temples and ears.

'Good, oh, very good indeed!' thought Aschenbach, assum-
ing the patronizing air of the connoisseur to hide, as artists will,
their ravishment over a masterpiece. 'Yes,' he went on to himself, 'if it were not that sea and beach were waiting for me, I
should sit here as long as you do.' But he went out on that,
passing through the hall, beneath the watchful eye of the functionaries, down the steps and directly across the board walk
to the section of the beach reserved for the guests of the hotel.
The bathing-master, a barefoot old man in linen trousers and
sailor blouse, with a straw hat, showed him the cabin that had
been rented for him, and Aschenbach had him set up table and
chair on the sandy platform before it. Then he dragged the
reclining-chair through the pale yellow sand, closer to the sea,
sat down, and composed himself.

He delighted, as always, in the scene on the beach, the sight
of sophisticated society giving itself over to a simple life at
the edge of the element. The shallow grey sea was already gay
with children wading, with swimmers, with figures in bright
colours lying on the sand-banks with arms behind their heads.
Some were rowing in little keelless boats painted red and blue,
and laughing when they capsized. A long row of *capanne* ran
down the beach, with platforms, where people sat as on veran-
das, and there was social life, with bustle and with indolent
repose; visits were paid, amid much chatter, punctilious morning toilettes hob-nobbed with comfortable and privileged
dishabille. On the hard wet sand close to the sea figures in
white bath-robes or loose wrappings in garish colours strolled
up and down. A mammoth sand-hill had been built up on
Aschenbach's right, the work of children, who had stuck it
full of tiny flags. Vendors of sea-shells, fruit, and cakes knelt
beside their wares spread out on the sand. A row of cabins on

the left stood obliquely to the others and to the sea, thus form-
ing the boundary of the enclosure on this side; and on the
little veranda in front of one of these a Russian family was
encamped; bearded men with strong white teeth, ripe, indolent women, a Fräulein from the Baltic provinces, who sat at
an easel painting the sea and tearing her hair in despair; two
ugly but good-natured children and an old maidservant in a
head-cloth, with the caressing, servile manner of the born
dependent. There they sat together in grateful enjoyment of
their blessings: constantly shouting at their romping children,
who paid not the slightest heed; making jokes in broken
Italian to the funny old man who sold them sweetmeats, kissing each other on the cheeks – no jot concerned that their
domesticity was overlooked.

'I'll stop,' thought Aschenbach. 'Where could it be better
than here?' With his hands clasped in his lap he let his eyes
swim in the wideness of the sea, his gaze lose focus, blur, and
grow vague in the misty immensity of space. His love of the
ocean had profound sources: the hard-worked artist's longing
for rest, his yearning to seek refuge from the thronging manifold shapes of his fancy in the bosom of the simple and vast;
and another yearning, opposed to his art and perhaps for that
very reason a lure, for the unorganized, the immeasurable,
the eternal – in short, for nothingness. He whose preoccupation is with excellence longs fervently to find rest in perfection; and is not nothingness a form of perfection? As he sat
there dreaming thus, deep, deep into the void, suddenly the
margin line of the shore was cut by a human form. He
gathered up his gaze and withdrew it from the illimitable,
and lo, it was the lovely boy who crossed his vision coming
from the left along the sand. He was barefoot, ready for
wading, the slender legs uncovered above the knee, and
moved slowly, yet with such a proud, light tread as to make
it seem he had never worn shoes. He looked towards the
diagonal row of cabins; and the sight of the Russian family,

leading their lives there in joyous simplicity, distorted his
features in a spasm of angry disgust. His brow darkened, his
lips curled, one corner of the mouth was drawn down in a
harsh line that marred the curve of the cheek, his frown was
so heavy that the eyes seemed to sink in as they uttered
beneath the black and vicious language of hate. He looked
down, looked threateningly back once more; then giving it
up with a violent and contemptuous shoulder-shrug, he left
his enemies in the rear.

A feeling of delicacy, a qualm, almost like a sense of shame,
made Aschenbach turn away as though he had not seen; he
felt unwilling to take advantage of having been, by chance,
privy to this passionate reaction. But he was in troth both
moved and exhilarated – that is to say, he was delighted. This
childish exhibition of fanaticism, directed against the good-
naturedest simplicity in the world – it gave to the godlike and
inexpressive the final human touch. The figure of the half-
grown lad, a masterpiece from nature's own hand, had been
significant enough when it gratified the eye alone; and now it
evoked sympathy as well – the little episode had set it off, lent
it a dignity in the onlooker's eyes that was beyond its years.

Aschenbach listened with still averted head to the boy's
voice announcing his coming to his companions at the sand-
heap. The voice was clear, though a little weak, but they
answered, shouting his name – or his nickname – again and
again. Aschenbach was not without curiosity to learn it, but
could make out nothing more exact than two musical syll-
ables, something like Adgio – or, often still, Adjiu, with a
long-drawn-out u at the end. He liked the melodious sound,
and found it fitting; said it over to himself a few times and
turned back with satisfaction to his papers.

Holding his travelling-pad on his knees, he took his foun-
tain-pen and began to answer various items of his correspondence. But presently he felt it too great a pity to turn his back,
and the eyes of his mind, for the sake of mere commonplace

correspondence, to this scene which was, after all, the most
rewarding one he knew. He put aside his papers and swung
round to the sea; in no long time, beguiled by the voices of
the children at play, he had turned his head and sat resting it
against the chair-back, while he gave himself up to contem-
plating the activities of the exquisite Adgio.

His eye found him at once, the red breast-knot was unmistakable. With some nine or ten companions, boys and girls of
his own age and younger, he was busy putting in place an old
plank to serve as a bridge across the ditches between the sand-
piles. He directed the work by shouting and motioning with
his head, and they were all chattering in many tongues –
French, Polish, and even some of the Balkan languages. But
his was the name oftenest on their lips, he was plainly sought
after, wooed, admired. One lad in particular, a Pole like himself, with a name that sounded something like Jaschiu, a sturdy
lad with brilliantined black hair, in a belted linen suit, was
his particular liegeman and friend. Operations at the sand-pile
being ended for the time, they two walked away along the
beach, with their arms round each other's waists, and once
the lad Jaschiu gave Adgio a kiss.

Aschenbach felt like shaking a finger at him. 'But you, Cri-
tobulus,' he thought with a smile, 'you I advise to take a year's
leave. That long, at least, you will need for complete recovery.'
A vendor came by with strawberries, and Aschenbach made
his second breakfast of the great luscious, dead-ripe fruit. It
had grown very warm, although the sun had not availed to
pierce the heavy layer of mist. His mind felt relaxed, his senses
revelled in this vast and soothing communion with the silence
of the sea. The grave and serious man found sufficient occupa-
tion in speculating what name it could be that sounded like
Adgio. And with the help of a few Polish memories he at
length fixed on Tadzio, a shortened form of Thaddeus, which
sounded, when called, like Tadziu or Adziu.

Tadzio was bathing. Aschenbach had lost sight of him for

a moment, then descried him far out in the water, which was
shallow a very long way – saw his head, and his arm striking
out like an oar. But his watchful family were already on the
alert; the mother and governess called from the veranda in
front of their bathing-cabin, until the lad's name, with its
softened consonants and long-drawn u-sound, seemed to pos-
sess the beach like a rallying-cry; the cadence had something
sweet and wild: 'Tadziu! Tadziu!' He turned and ran back
against the water, churning the waves to a foam, his head
flung high. The sight of this living figure, virginally pure and
austere, with dripping locks, beautiful as a tender young god,
emerging from the depths of sea and sky, outrunning the
element – it conjured up mythologies, it was like a primeval
legend, handed down from the beginning of time, of the
birth of form, of the origin of the gods. With closed lids
Aschenbach listened to this poesy hymning itself silently
within him, and anon he thought it was good to be here and
that he would stop awhile.

Afterwards Tadzio lay on the sand and rested from his
bathe, wrapped in his white sheet, which he wore drawn
underneath the right shoulder, so that his head was cradled
on his bare right arm. And even when Aschenbach read, without looking up, he was conscious that the lad was there; that
it would cost him but the slightest turn of the head to have
the rewarding vision once more in his purview. Indeed, it was
almost as though he sat there to guard the youth's repose;
occupied, of course, with his own affairs, yet alive to the
presence of that noble human creature close at hand. And his
heart was stirred, it felt a father's kindness: such an emotion
as the possessor of beauty can inspire in one who has offered
himself up in spirit to create beauty.

At midday he left the beach, returned to the hotel, and was
carried up in the lift to his room. There he lingered a little
time before the glass and looked at his own grey hair, his
keen and weary face. And he thought of his fame, and how

people gazed respectfully at him in the streets, on account of
his unerring gift of words and their power to charm. He
called up all the worldly successes his genius had reaped, all
he could remember, even his patent of nobility. Then went
to luncheon down in the dining-room, sat at his little table
and ate. Afterwards he mounted again in the lift, and a group
of young folk, Tadzio among them, pressed with him into
the little compartment. It was the first time Aschenbach-had
seen him close at hand, not merely in perspective, and could
see and take account of the details of his humanity. Someone
spoke to the lad, and he, answering, with indescribably lovely
smile, stepped out again, as they had come to the first floor,
backwards, with his eyes cast down. 'Beauty makes people
self-conscious,' Aschenbach thought, and considered within
himself imperatively why this should be. He had noted, further, that Tadzio's teeth were imperfect, rather jagged and
bluish, without a healthy glaze, and of that peculiar brittle
transparency which the teeth of chlorotic people often show.
'He is delicate, he is sickly,' Aschenbach thought. 'He will
most likely not live to grow old.' He did not try to account
for the pleasure the idea gave him.

   In the afternoon he spent two hours in his room, then took
the *vaporetto* to Venice, across the foul-smelling lagoon. He
got out at San Marco, had his tea in the Piazza, and then, as
his custom was, took a walk through the streets. But this walk
of his brought about nothing less than a revolution in his
mood and an entire change in all his plans.

   There was a hateful sultriness in the narrow streets. The air
was so heavy that all the manifold smells wafted out of houses,
shops, and cook-shops – smells of oil, perfumery, and so forth
– hung low, like exhalations, not dissipating. Cigarette smoke
seemed to stand in the air, it drifted so slowly away. To-day
the crowd in these narrow lanes oppressed the stroller instead
of diverting him. The longer he walked, the more was he in
tortures under that state, which is the product of the sea air

and the sirocco and which excites and enervates at once. He perspired painfully. His eyes rebelled, his chest was heavy, he felt feverish, the blood throbbed in his temples. He fled from the huddled, narrow streets of the commercial city, crossed many bridges, and came into the poor quarter of Venice. Beggars waylaid him, the canals sickened him with their evil exhalations. He reached a quiet square, one of those that exist at the city's heart, forsaken of God and man; there he rested awhile on the margin of a fountain, wiped his brow, and admitted to himself that he must be gone.

For the second time, and now quite definitely, the city proved that in certain weathers it could be directly inimical to his health. Nothing but sheer unreasoning obstinacy would linger on, hoping for an unprophesiable change in the wind. A quick decision was in place. He could not go home at this stage, neither summer nor winter quarters would be ready. But Venice had not a monopoly of sea and shore: there were other spots where these were to be had without the evil concomitants of lagoon and fever-breeding vapours. He remembered a little bathing-place not far from Trieste of which he had had a good report. Why not go thither? At once, of course, in order that this second change might be worth the making. He resolved, he rose to his feet and sought the nearest gondola-landing, where he took a boat and was conveyed to San Marco through the gloomy windings of many canals, beneath balconies of delicate marble traceries flanked by carven lions; round slippery corners of wall, past melancholy façades with ancient business shields reflected in the rocking water. It was not too easy to arrive at his destination, for his gondolier, being in league with various lace-makers and glass-blowers, did his best to persuade his fare to pause, look, and be tempted to buy. Thus the charm of this bizarre passage through the heart of Venice, even while it played upon his spirit, yet was sensibly cooled by the predatory commercial spirit of the fallen queen of the seas.

Once back in his hotel, he announced at the office, even before dinner, that circumstances unforeseen obliged him to leave early next morning. The management expressed its regret, it changed his money and receipted his bill. He dined, and spent the luke-warm evening in a rocking-chair on the rear terrace, reading the newspapers. Before he went to bed, he made his luggage ready against the morning.

His sleep was not of the best, for the prospect of another journey made him restless. When he opened his window next morning, the sky was still overcast, but the air seemed fresher – and there and then his rue began. Had he not given notice too soon? Had he not let himself be swayed by a slight and momentary indisposition? If he had only been patient, not lost heart so quickly, tried to adapt himself to the climate, or even waited for a change in the weather before deciding! Then, instead of the hurry and flurry of departure, he would have before him now a morning like yesterday's on the beach. Too late! He must go on wanting what he had wanted yesterday. He dressed and at eight o'clock went down to breakfast.

When he entered the breakfast-room it was empty. Guests came in while he sat waiting for his order to be filled. As he sipped his tea he saw the Polish girls enter with their governess, chaste and morning-fresh, with sleep-reddened eyelids. They crossed the room and sat down at their table in the window. Behind them came the porter, cap in hand, to announce that it was time for him to go. The car was waiting to convey him and other travellers to the Hôtel Excelsior, whence they would go by motor-boat through the company's private canal to the station. Time pressed. But Aschenbach found it did nothing of the sort. There still lacked more than an hour of train-time. He felt irritated at the hotel habit of getting the guests out of the house earlier than necessary; and requested the porter to let him breakfast in peace. The man hesitated and withdrew, only to come back again five minutes later. The car could wait no longer. Good, then it

might go, and take his trunk with it, Aschenbach answered
with some heat. He would use the public conveyance, in his
own time; he begged them to leave the choice of it to him.
The functionary bowed. Aschenbach, pleased to be rid of
him, made a leisurely meal, and even had a newspaper of the
waiter. When at length he rose, the time was grown very
short. And it so happened that at that moment Tadzio came
through the glass doors into the room.

To reach his own table he crossed the traveller's path, and
modestly cast down his eyes before the grey-haired man of
the lofty brows – only to lift them again in that sweet way
he had and direct his full soft gaze upon Aschenbach's face.
Then he was past. 'For the last time, Tadzio,' thought the
elder man. 'It was all too brief!' Quite unusually for him, he
shaped a farewell with his lips, he actually uttered it, and
added: 'May God bless you!' Then he went out, distributed
tips, exchanged farewells with the mild little manager in the
frock-coat, and, followed by the porter with his hand-luggage,
left the hotel. On foot as he had come, he passed through the
white-blossoming avenue, diagonally across the island to the
boat-landing. He went on board at once – but the tale of his
journey across the lagoon was a tale of woe, a passage through
the very valley of regrets.

It was the well-known route: through the lagoon, past San
Marco, up the Grand Canal. Aschenbach sat on the circular
bench in the bows, with his elbow on the railing, one hand
shading his eyes. They passed the Public Gardens, once more
the princely charm of the Piazzetta rose up before him and
then dropped behind, next came the great row of palaces,
the canal curved, and the splendid marble arches of the Rialto
came in sight. The traveller gazed – and his bosom was torn.
The atmosphere of the city, the faintly rotten scent of swamp
and sea, which had driven him to leave – in what deep, tender,
almost painful draughts he breathed it in! How was it he had
not known, had not thought, how much his heart was set

upon it all! What this morning had been slight regret, some
little doubt of his own wisdom, turned now to grief, to
actual wretchedness, a mental agony so sharp that it repeat-
edly brought tears to his eyes, while he questioned himself
how he could have foreseen it. The hardest part, the part that
more than once it seemed he could not bear, was the thought
that he should never more see Venice again. Since now for
the second time the place had made him ill, since for the
second time he had had to flee for his life, he must henceforth
regard it as a forbidden spot, to be forever shunned; senseless
to try it again, after he had proved himself unfit. Yes, if he
fled it now, he felt that wounded pride must prevent his
return to this spot where twice he had made actual bodily
surrender. And this conflict between inclination and capacity
all at once assumed, in this middle-aged man's mind, immense
weight and importance; the physical defeat seemed a shameful
thing, to be avoided at whatever cost; and he stood amazed
at the ease with which on the day before he had yielded to it.

Meanwhile the steamer neared the station landing; his
anguish of irresolution amounted almost to panic. To leave
seemed to the sufferer impossible, to remain not less so. Torn
thus between two alternatives, he entered the station. It was
very late, he had not a moment to lose. Time pressed, it
scourged him onward. He hastened to buy his ticket and
looked round in the crowd to find the hotel porter. The man
appeared and said that the trunk had already gone off. 'Gone
already?' 'Yes, it has gone to Como.' 'To Como?' A hasty
exchange of words – angry questions from Aschenbach, and
puzzled replies from the porter – at length made it clear that
the trunk had been put with the wrong luggage even before
leaving the hotel, and in company with other trunks was now
well on its way in precisely the wrong direction.

Aschenbach found it hard to wear the right expression as
he heard this news. A reckless joy, a deep incredible mirthful-
ness shook him almost as with a spasm. The porter dashed off

after the lost trunk, returning very soon, of course, to announce that his efforts were unavailing. Aschenbach said he
would not travel without his luggage; that he would go back
and wait at the Hôtel des Bains until it turned up. Was the
company's motor-boat still outside? The man said yes, it was
at the door. With his native eloquence he prevailed upon the
ticket-agent to take back the ticket already purchased; he
swore that he would wire, that no pains should be spared,
that the trunk would be restored in the twinkling of an eye.
And the unbelievable thing came to pass; the traveller, twenty
minutes after he had reached the station, found himself once
more on the Grand Canal on his way back to the Lido.

What a strange adventure indeed, this right-about face of
destiny – incredible, humiliating, whimsical as any dream!
To be passing again, within the hour, these scenes from which
in profoundest grief he had but now taken leave forever! The
little swift-moving vessel, a furrow of foam at its prow, tack-
ing with droll agility between steamboats and gondolas, went
like a shot to its goal; and he, its sole passenger, sat hiding the
panic and thrills of a truant schoolboy beneath a mask of
forced resignation. His breast still heaved from time to time
with a burst of laughter over the contretemps. Things could
not, he told himself, have fallen out more luckily. There would
be the necessary explanations, a few astonished faces – then
all would be well once more, a mischance prevented, a griev-
ous error set right; and all he had thought to have left forever
was his own once more, his for as long as he liked. . . . And
did the boat's swift motion deceive him, or was the wind now
coming from the sea?

The waves struck against the tiled sides of the narrow canal.
At Hôtel Excelsior the automobile omnibus awaited the returned traveller and bore him along by the crisping waves
back to the Hôtel des Bains. The little mustachioed manager
in the frock-coat came down the steps to greet him.

In dulcet tones he deplored the mistake, said how painful

it was to the management and himself; applauded Aschenbach's resolve to stop on until the errant trunk came back; his former room, alas, was already taken, but another as good awaited his approval. '*Pas de chance, monsieur,*' said the Swiss lift-porter, with a smile, as he conveyed him upstairs. And the fugitive was soon quartered in another room which in situation and furnishings almost precisely resembled the first.

He laid out the contents of his hand-bag in their wonted places; then, tired out, dazed by the whirl of the extraordinary forenoon, subsided into the arm-chair by the open window. The sea wore a pale-green cast, the air felt thinner and purer, the beach with its cabins and boats had more colour, notwithstanding the sky was still grey. Aschenbach, his hands folded in his lap, looked out. He felt rejoiced to be back, yet displeased with his vacillating moods, his ignorance of his own real desires. Thus for nearly an hour he sat, dreaming, resting, barely thinking. At midday he saw Tadzio, in his striped sailor suit with red breast-knot, coming up from the sea, across the barrier and along the board walk to the hotel. Aschenbach recognized him, even at this height, knew it was he before he actually saw him, had it in mind to say to himself: 'Well, Tadzio, so here you are again too!' But the casual greeting died away before it reached his lips, slain by the truth in his heart. He felt the rapture of his blood, the poignant pleasure, and realized that it was for Tadzio's sake the leavetaking had been so hard.

He sat quite still, unseen at his high post, and looked within himself. His features were lively, he lifted his brows; a smile, alert, inquiring, vivid, widened the mouth. Then he raised his head, and with both hands, hanging limp over the chairarms, he described a slow motion, palms outward, a lifting and turning movement, as though to indicate a wide embrace. It was a gesture of welcome, a calm and deliberate acceptance of what might come.

Now daily the naked god with cheeks aflame drove his four

fire-breathing steeds through heaven's spaces; and with him streamed the strong east wind that fluttered his yellow locks. A sheen, like white satin, lay over all the idly rolling sea's expanse. The sand was burning hot. Awnings of rust-coloured canvas were spanned before the bathing-huts, under the ether's quivering silver-blue; one spent the morning hours within the small, sharp square of shadow they purveyed. But evening too was rarely lovely: balsamic with the breath of flowers and shrubs from the near-by park, while overhead the constellations circled in their spheres, and the murmuring of the night-girded sea swelled softly up and whispered to the soul. Such nights as these contained the joyful promise of a sunlit morrow, brim-full of sweetly ordered idleness, studded thick with countless precious possibilities.

The guest detained here by so happy a mischance was far from finding the return of his luggage a ground for setting out anew. For two days he had suffered slight inconvenience and had to dine in the large salon in his travelling clothes. Then the lost trunk was set down in his room, and he hastened to unpack, filling presses and drawers with his possessions. He meant to stay on – and on; he rejoiced in the prospect of wearing a silk suit for the hot morning hours on the beach and appearing in acceptable evening dress at dinner.

He was quick to fall in with the pleasing monotony of this manner of life, readily enchanted by its mild soft brilliance and ease. And what a spot it is, indeed! – uniting the charms of a luxurious bathing-resort by a southern sea with the immediate nearness of a unique and marvellous city. Aschenbach was not pleasure-loving. Always, wherever and whenever it was the order of the day to be merry, to refrain from labour and make glad the heart, he would soon be conscious of the imperative summons – and especially was this so in his youth – back to the high fatigues, the sacred and fasting service that consumed his days. This spot and this alone had power to beguile him, to relax his resolution, to make him glad. At times

– of a forenoon perhaps, as he lay in the shadow of his awning, gazing out dreamily over the blue of the southern sea, or in the mildness of the night, beneath the wide starry sky, ensconced among the cushions of the gondola that bore him Lido-wards after an evening on the Piazza, while the gay lights faded and the melting music of the serenades died away on his ear – he would think of his mountain home, the theatre of his summer labours. There clouds hung low and trailed through the garden, violent storms extinguished the lights of the house at night, and the ravens he fed swung in the tops of the fir trees. And he would feel transported to Elysium, to the ends of the earth, to a spot most carefree for the sons of men, where no snow is, and no winter, no storms or downpours of rain; where Oceanus sends a mild and cooling breath, and days flow on in blissful idleness, without effort or struggle, entirely dedicate to the sun and the feasts of the sun.

Aschenbach saw the boy Tadzio almost constantly. The narrow confines of their world of hotel and beach, the daily round followed by all alike, brought him in close, almost uninterrupted touch with the beautiful lad. He encountered him everywhere – in the salons of the hotel, on the cooling rides to the city and back, among the splendours of the Piazza, and besides all this in many another going and coming as chance vouchsafed. But it was the regular morning hours on the beach which gave him his happiest opportunity to study and admire the lovely apparition. Yes, this immediate happiness, this daily recurring boon at the hand of circumstance, this it was that filled him with content, with joy in life, enriched his stay, and lingered out the row of sunny days that fell into place so pleasantly one behind the other.

He rose early – as early as though he had a panting press of work – and was among the first on the beach, when the sun was still benign and the sea dazzling white in its morning slumber. He gave the watchman a friendly good-morning and chatted with the barefoot, white-haired old man who pre-

pared his place, spread the awning, trundled out the chair and
table on to the little platform. Then he settled down; he had
three or four hours before the sun reached its height and the
fearful climax of its power; three or four hours while the sea
went deeper and deeper blue; three or four hours in which to
watch Tadzio.

He would see him coming up, on the left, along the margin
of the sea; or from behind, between the cabins; or, with a
start of joyful surprise, would discover that he himself was
late, and Tadzio already down, in the blue and white bathing-
suit that was now his only wear on the beach; there and en-
grossed in his usual activities in the sand, beneath the sun. It was
a sweetly idle, trifling, fitful life, of play and rest, of strolling,
wading, digging, fishing, swimming, lying on the sand. Often
the women sitting on the platform would call out to him in
their high voices: 'Tadziu! Tadziu!' and he would come run-
ning and waving his arms, eager to tell them what he had
found, what caught – shells, seahorses, jelly-fish, and side-
wards-running crabs. Aschenbach understood not a word he
said; it might be the sheerest commonplace, in his ear it became mingled harmonies. Thus the lad's foreign birth raised
his speech to music; a wanton sun showered splendour on
him, and the noble distances of the sea formed the background
which set off his figure.

Soon the observer knew every line and pose of this form
that limned itself so freely against sea and sky; its every loveliness, though conned by heart, yet thrilled him each day afresh;
his admiration knew no bounds, the delight of his eye was
unending. Once the lad was summoned to speak to a guest
who was waiting for his mother at their cabin. He ran up, ran
dripping wet out of the sea, tossing his curls, and put out his
hand, standing with his weight on one leg, resting the other
foot on the toes; as he stood there in a posture of suspense the
turn of his body was enchanting, while his features wore a
look half shamefaced, half conscious of the duty breeding laid

upon him to please. Or he would lie at full length, with his bath-robe around him, one slender young arm resting on the sand, his chin in the hollow of his hand; the lad they called Jaschiu squatting beside him, paying him court. There could be nothing lovelier on earth than the smile and look with which the playmate thus singled out rewarded his humble friend and vassal. Again, he might be at the water's edge, alone, removed from his family, quite close to Aschenbach; standing erect, his hands clasped at the back of his neck, rocking slowly on the balls of his feet, day-dreaming away into blue space, while little waves ran up and bathed his toes. The ringlets of honey-coloured hair clung to his temples and neck, the fine down along the upper vertebrae was yellow in the sunlight; the thin envelope of flesh covering the torso betrayed the delicate outlines of the ribs and the symmetry of the breast-structure. His armpits were still as smooth as a statue's, smooth the glistening hollows behind the knees, where the blue network of veins suggested that the body was formed of some stuff more transparent than mere flesh. What discipline, what precision of thought were expressed by the tense youthful perfection of this form! And yet the pure, strong will which had laboured in darkness and succeeded in bringing this godlike work of art to the light of day – was it not known and familiar to him, the artist? Was not the same force at work in himself when he strove in cold fury to liberate from the marble mass of language the slender forms of his art which he saw with the eye of his mind and would body forth to men as the mirror and image of spiritual beauty?

Mirror and image! His eyes took in the proud bearing of that figure there at the blue water's edge; with an outburst of rapture he told himself that what he saw was beauty's very essence; form as divine thought, the single and pure perfection which resides in the mind, of which an image and likeness, rare and holy, was here raised up for adoration. This was very frenzy – and without a scruple, nay, eagerly, the ageing artist bade it come. His mind was in travail, his whole mental background in a state of flux. Memory flung up in him the primitive thoughts which are youth's inheritance, but which with him had remained latent, never leaping up into a blaze. Has it not been written that the sun beguiles our attention from things of the intellect to fix it on things of the sense? The sun, they say, dazzles; so bewitching reason and memory that the soul for very pleasure forgets its actual state, to cling with doting on the loveliest of all the objects she shines on. Yes, and then it is only through the medium of some corporeal being that it can raise itself again to contemplation of higher things. Amor, in sooth, is like the mathematician who in order to give children a knowledge of pure form must do so in the language of pictures; so, too, the god, in order to make visible the spirit, avails himself of the forms and colours of human youth, gilding it with all imaginable beauty that it may serve memory as a tool, the very sight of which then sets us afire with pain and longing.

Such were the devotee's thoughts, such the power of his emotions. And the sea, so bright with glancing sunbeams, wove in his mind a spell and summoned up a lovely picture: there was the ancient plane-tree outside the walls of Athens, a hallowed, shady spot, fragrant with willow-blossom and adorned with images and votive offerings in honour of the nymphs and Achelous. Clear ran the smooth-pebbled stream at the foot of the spreading tree. Crickets were fiddling. But on the gentle grassy slope, where one could lie yet hold the head erect, and shelter from the scorching heat, two men reclined, an elder with a younger, ugliness paired with beauty and wisdom with grace. Here Socrates held forth to youthful Phaedrus upon the nature of virtue and desire, wooing him with insinuating wit and charming turns of phrase. He told him of the shuddering and unwonted heat that comes upon him whose heart is open, when his eye beholds an image of eternal beauty; spoke of the impious and corrupt, who cannot conceive beauty though they see its image, and are incapable of awe; and of the fear and reverence felt by the noble soul when he beholds a godlike face or a form which is a good image of beauty: how as he gazes he worships the beautiful one and scarcely dares to look upon him, but would offer sacrifice as to an idol or a god, did he not fear to be thought stark mad. 'For beauty, my Phaedrus, beauty alone, is lovely and visible at once. For, mark you, it is the sole aspect of the spiritual which we can perceive through our senses, or bear so to perceive. Else what should become of us, if the divine, if reason and virtue and truth, were to speak to us through the senses? Should we not perish and be consumed by love, as Semele aforetime was by Zeus? So beauty, then, is the beauty-lover's way to the spirit – but only the way, only the means, my little Phaedrus.' ... And then, sly arch-lover that he was, he said the subtlest thing of all: that the lover was nearer the divine than the beloved; for the god was in the one but not in the other – perhaps the tenderest, most mocking thought that ever was thought, and source of all the guile and secret bliss the lover knows.

Thought that can emerge wholly into feeling, feeling that can merge wholly into thought – these are the artist's highest joy. And our solitary felt in himself at this moment power to command and wield a thought that thrilled with emotion, an emotion as precise and concentrated as thought: namely, that nature herself shivers with ecstasy when the mind bows down in homage before beauty. He felt a sudden desire to write. Eros, indeed, we are told, loves idleness, and for idle hours alone was he created. But in this crisis the violence of our sufferer's seizure was directed almost wholly towards production, its occasion almost a matter of indifference. News had reached him on his travels that a certain problem had been raised, the intellectual world challenged for its opinion on a great and burning question of art and taste. By nature and experience the theme was his own: and he could not resist the temptation to set it off in the glistering foil of his words. He would write, and moreover he would write in Tadzio's presence. This lad should be in a sense his model, his style should follow the lines of this figure that seemed to him divine; he would snatch up this beauty into the realms of the mind, as once the eagle bore the Trojan shepherd aloft. Never had the pride of the word been so sweet to him, never had he known so well that Eros is in the word, as in those perilous and precious hours when he sat at his rude table, within the shade of his awning, his idol full in his view and the music of his voice in his ears, and fashioned his little essay after the model Tadzio's beauty set: that page and a half of choicest prose, so chaste, so lofty, so poignant with feeling, which would shortly be the wonder and admiration of the multitude. Verily it is well for the world that it sees only the beauty of the completed work and not its origins nor the conditions whence it sprang; since knowledge of the artist's inspiration might often but confuse and alarm and so prevent the full effect of its excellence. Strange hours, indeed, these were, and strangely unnerving the labour that filled them! Strangely fruitful intercourse this, between one body and another mind! When Aschenbach put aside his work and left the beach he felt exhausted, he felt broken — conscience reproached him, as it were after a debauch.

Next morning on leaving the hotel he stood at the top of the stairs leading down from the terrace and saw Tadzio in front of him on his way to the beach. The lad had just reached the gate in the railings, and he was alone. Aschenbach felt, quite simply, a wish to overtake him, to address him and have the pleasure of his reply and answering look; to put upon a blithe and friendly footing his relation with this being who all unconsciously had so greatly heightened and quickened his emotions. The lovely youth moved at a loitering pace — he might be easily overtaken; and Aschenbach hastened his own step. He reached him on the board walk that ran behind the bathing-cabins, and all but put out his hand to lay it on shoulder or head, while his lips parted to utter a friendly salutation in French. But – perhaps from the swift pace of his last few steps – he found his heart throbbing unpleasantly fast, while his breath came in such quick pants that he could only have gasped had he tried to speak. He hesitated, sought after self-control, was suddenly panic-stricken lest the boy notice him hanging there behind him and look round. Then he gave up, abandoned his plan, and passed him with bent head and hurried step.

'Too late! Too late!' he thought as he went by. But was it too late? This step he had delayed to take might so easily have put everything in a lighter key, have led to a sane recovery from his folly. But the truth may have been that the ageing man did not want to be cured, that his illusion was far too dear to him. Who shall unriddle the puzzle of the artist nature? Who understands that mingling of discipline and licence in which it stands so deeply rooted? For not to be able to want sobriety is licentious folly. Aschenbach was no longer disposed to self-analysis. He had no taste for it; his self-esteem, the attitude of mind proper to his years, his maturity and single-mindedness, disinclined him to look within himself and decide whether it was constraint or puerile sensuality that had prevented him from carrying out his project. He felt confused, he was afraid someone, if only the watchman, might have been observing his behaviour and final surrender – very much he feared being ridiculous. And all the time he was laughing at himself for his serio-comic seizure. 'Quite crestfallen,' he thought. 'I was like the gamecock that lets his wings droop in the battle. That must be the Love-God himself, that makes us hang our heads at sight of beauty and weighs our proud spirits low as the ground.' Thus he played with the idea – he embroidered upon it, and was too arrogant to admit fear of an emotion.

The term he had set for his holiday passed by unheeded; he had no thought of going home. Ample funds had been sent him. His sole concern was that the Polish family might leave and a chance question put to the hotel barber elicited the information that they had come only very shortly before himself. The sun browned his face and hands, the invigorating salty air heightened his emotional energies. Heretofore he had wont to give out at once, in some new effort, the powers accumulated by sleep or food or outdoor air; but now the strength that flowed in upon him with each day of sun and sea and idleness he let go up in one extravagant gush of emotional intoxication.

His sleep was fitful; the priceless, equable days were divided one from the next by brief nights filled with happy unrest. He went, indeed, early to bed, for at nine o'clock, with the departure of Tadzio from the scene, the day was over for him. But in the faint greyness of the morning a tender pang would go through him as his heart was minded of its adventure; he could no longer bear his pillow and rising, would wrap himself against the early chill and sit down by the window to await the sunrise. Awe of the miracle filled his soul new-risen from its sleep. Heaven, earth, and its waters yet lay enfolded in the ghostly, glassy pallor of dawn; one paling star still swam in the shadowy vast. But there came a breath, a winged word from far and inaccessible abodes, that Eos was rising from the side of her spouse, and there was that first sweet reddening of the farthest strip of sea and sky that manifests creation to man's sense. She neared, the goddess, ravisher of youth, who stole away Cleitos and Cephalus and, defying all the envious Olympians, tasted beautiful Orion's love. At the world's edge began a strewing of roses, a shining and a blooming ineffably pure; baby cloudlets hung illuminated, like attendant amoretti, in the blue and blushful haze; purple effulgence fell upon the sea, that seemed to heave it forward on its welling waves; from horizon to zenith went quivering thrusts like golden lances, the gleam became a glare; without a sound, with godlike violence, glow and glare and rolling flames streamed upwards, and with flying hoof-beats the steeds of the sun-god mounted the sky. The lonely watcher sat, the splendour of the god shone on him, he closed his eyes and let the glory kiss his lids. Forgotten feelings, precious pangs of his youth, quenched long since by the stern service that had been his life and now returned so strangely metamorphosed – he recognized them with a puzzled, wondering smile. He mused, he dreamed, his lips slowly shaped a name; still smiling, his face turned seawards and his hands lying folded in his lap, he fell asleep once more as he sat.

But that day, which began so fierily and festally, was not like other days; it was transmuted and gilded with mythical significance. For whence could come the breath, so mild and meaningful, like a whisper from higher spheres, that played about temple and ear? Troops of small feathery white clouds ranged over the sky, like grazing herds of the gods. A stronger wind arose, and Poseidon's horses ran up, arching their manes, among them too the steers of him with the purpled locks, who lowered their horns and bellowed as they came on; while like prancing goats the waves on the farther strand leaped among the craggy rocks. It was a world possessed, peopled by Pan, that closed round the spellbound man, and his doting heart conceived the most delicate fancies. When the sun was going down behind Venice, he would sometimes sit on a bench in the park and watch Tadzio, white-clad, with gay-coloured sash, at play there on the rolled gravel with his ball; and at such times it was not Tadzio whom he saw, but Hyacinthus, doomed to die because two gods were rivals for his love. Ah, yes, he tasted the envious pangs that Zephyr knew when his rival, bow and cithara, oracle and all forgot, played with the beauteous youth; he watched the discus, guided by torturing jealousy, strike the beloved head; paled as he received the broken body in his arms, and saw the flower spring up, watered by that sweet blood and signed for evermore with his lament.

There can be no relation more strange, more critical, than that between two beings who know each other only with their eyes, who meet daily, yes, even hourly, eye each other with a fixed regard, and yet by some whim or freak of convention feel constrained to act like strangers. Uneasiness rules between them, unslaked curiosity, a hysterical desire to give rein to their suppressed impulse to recognize and address each other; even, actually, a sort of strained but mutual regard. For one human being instinctively feels respect and love for another human being so long as he does not know him well enough to judge him; and that he does not, the craving he feels is evidence.

Some sort of relationship and acquaintanceship was perforce set up between Aschenbach and the youthful Tadzio; it was with a thrill of joy the older man perceived that the lad was not entirely unresponsive to all the tender notice lavished on him. For instance, what should move the lovely youth, nowadays when he descended to the beach, always to avoid the board walk behind the bathing-huts and saunter along the sand, passing Aschenbach's tent in front, sometimes so unnecessarily close as almost to graze his table or chair? Could the power of an emotion so beyond his own so draw, so fascinate its innocent object? Daily Aschenbach would wait for Tadzio. Then sometimes, on his approach, he would pretend to be preoccupied and let the charmer pass unregarded by. But sometimes he looked up, and their glances met; when that happened both were profoundly serious. The elder's dignified and cultured mien let nothing appear of his inward state; but in Tadzio's eyes a question lay – he faltered in his step, gazed on the ground, then up again with that ineffably sweet look he had; and when he was past, something in his bearing seemed to say that only good breeding hindered him from turning round.

But once, one evening, it fell out differently. The Polish brother and sisters, with their governess, had missed the evening meal, and Aschenbach had noted the fact with concern. He was restive over their absence, and after dinner walked up and down in front of the hotel, in evening dress and a straw hat; when suddenly he saw the nunlike sisters with their companion appear in the light of the arc-lamps, and four paces behind them Tadzio. Evidently they came from the steamer-landing, having dined for some reason in Venice. It had been chilly on the lagoon, for Tadzio wore a dark-blue reefer-jacket with gilt buttons, and a cap to match. Sun and sea air could not burn his skin, it was the same creamy marble hue as at first - though he did look a little pale, either from the cold or in the bluish moonlight of the arc-lamps. The shapely brows were so delicately drawn, the eyes so deeply dark – lovelier he was than words could say, and as often the thought visited Aschenbach, and brought its own pang, that language could but extol, not reproduce, the beauties of the sense.

The sight of that dear form was unexpected, it had appeared unhoped-for, without giving him time to compose his features. Joy, surprise, and admiration might have painted themselves quite openly upon his face – and just at this second it happened that Tadzio smiled. Smiled at Aschenbach, unabashed and friendly, a speaking, winning, captivating smile, with slowly parting lips. With such a smile it might be that Narcissus bent over the mirroring pool, a smile profound, infatuated, lingering, as he put out his arms to the reflection of his own beauty; the lips just slightly pursed, perhaps half-realizing his own folly in trying to kiss the cold lips of his shadow – with a mingling of coquetry and curiosity and a faint unease, enthralling and enthralled.

Aschenbach received that smile and turned away with it as though entrusted with a fatal gift. So shaken was he that he had to flee from the lighted terrace and front gardens and seek out with hurried steps the darkness of the park at the rear. Reproaches strangely mixed of tenderness and remonstrance burst from him: 'How dare you smile like that! No one is allowed to smile like that!' He flung himself on a bench, his composure gone to the winds, and breathed in the nocturnal fragrance of the garden. He leaned back, with hanging arms, quivering from head to foot, and quite unmanned he whispered the hackneyed phrase of love and longing – impossible in these circumstances, absurd, abject, ridiculous enough, yet sacred too, and not unworthy of honour even here: 'I love you!'

In the fourth week of his stay on the Lido, Gustave von Aschenbach made certain singular observations touching the world about him. He noticed, in the first place, that though the season was approaching its height, yet the number of guests declined and, in particular, that the German tongue had suffered a rout, being scarcely or never heard in the land. At table and on the beach he caught nothing but foreign words. One day at the barber's – where he was now a frequent visitor – he heard something rather startling. The barber mentioned a German family who had just left the Lido after a brief stay, and rattled on in his obsequious way: 'The signore is not leaving – he has no fear of the sickness, has he?' Aschenbach looked at him. 'The sickness?' he repeated. Whereat the prattler fell silent, became very busy all at once, affected not to hear. When Aschenbach persisted he said he really knew nothing at all about it, and tried in a fresh burst of eloquence to drown the embarrassing subject.

That was one forenoon. After luncheon, Aschenbach had himself ferried across to Venice, in a dead calm, under a burning sun; driven by his mania, he was following the Polish young folk, whom he had seen with their companion, taking the way to the landing-stage. He did not find his idol on the Piazza. But as he sat there at tea, at a little round table on the shady side, suddenly he noticed a peculiar odour, which, it seemed to him now, had been in the air for days without his being aware: a sweetish, medicinal smell, associated with wounds and disease and suspect cleanliness. He sniffed and

pondered and at length recognized it; finished his tea and left
the square at the end facing the cathedral. In the narrow space
the stench grew stronger. At the street corners placards were
stuck up, in which the city authorities warned the population
against the danger of certain infections of the gastric system,
prevalent during the heated season; advising them not to eat
oysters or other shell-fish and not to use the canal waters. The
ordinance showed every sign of minimizing an existing situation. Little groups of people stood about silently in the squares
and on the bridges; the traveller moved among them, watched
and listened and thought.

He spoke to a shopkeeper lounging at his door among dang-
ling coral necklaces and trinkets of artificial amethyst, and
asked him about the disagreeable odour. The man looked at
him, heavy-eyed, and hastily pulled himself together. 'Just a
formal precaution, signore,' he said, with a gesture. 'A police
regulation we have to put up with. The air is sultry – the
sirocco is not wholesome, as the signore knows. Just a precautionary measure, you understand – probably unnecessary.
. . .' Aschenbach thanked him and passed on. And on the
boat that bore him back to the Lido he smelt the germicide
again.

On reaching his hotel he sought the table in the lobby and
buried himself in the newspapers. The foreign-language sheets
had nothing. But in the German papers certain rumours were
mentioned, statistics given, then officially denied, then the
good faith of the denials called in question. The departure of
the German and Austrian contingent was thus made plain. As
for other nationals, they knew or suspected nothing – they
were still undisturbed. Aschenbach tossed the newspapers back
on the table. 'It ought to be kept quiet,' he thought, aroused.
'It should not be talked about.' And he felt in his heart a
curious elation at these events impending in the world about
him. Passion is like crime: it does not thrive on the established
order and the common round; it welcomes every blow dealt

the bourgeois structure, every weakening of the social fabric, because therein it feels a sure hope of its own advantage. These things that were going on in the unclean alleys of Venice, under cover of an official hushing-up policy – they gave Aschenbach a dark satisfaction. The city's evil secret mingled with the one in the depths of his heart – and he would have staked all he possessed to keep it, since in his infatuation he cared for nothing but to keep Tadzio here, and owned to himself, not without horror, that he could not exist were the lad to pass from his sight.

He was no longer satisfied to owe his communion with his charmer to chance and the routine of hotel life; he had begun to follow and waylay him. On Sundays, for example, the Polish family never appeared on the beach. Aschenbach guessed they went to mass at San Marco and pursued them thither. He passed from the glare of the Piazza into the golden twilight of the holy place and found him he sought bowed in worship over a prie-dieu. He kept in the background, standing on the fissured mosaic pavement among the devout populace, that knelt and muttered and made the sign of the cross; and the crowded splendour of the oriental temple weighed voluptuously on his sense. A heavily ornate priest intoned and gesticulated before the altar, where little candle-flames flickered helplessly in the reek of incense-breathing smoke; and with that cloying sacrificial smell another seemed to mingle – the odour of the sickened city. But through all the glamour and glitter, Aschenbach saw the exquisite creature there in front turn his head, seek out and meet his lover's eye.

The crowd streamed out through the portals into the brilliant square thick with fluttering doves, and the fond fool stood aside in the vestibule on the watch. He saw the Polish family leave the church. The children took ceremonial leave of their mother, and she turned towards the Piazzetta on her way home, while his charmer and the cloistered sisters, with their governess, passed beneath the clock tower into the

Merceria. When they were a few paces on, he followed – he stole behind them on their walk through the city. When they paused, he did so too; when they turned round, he fled into inns and courtyards to let them pass. Once he lost them from view, hunted feverishly over bridges and in filthy *culs-de-sac*, only to confront them suddenly in a narrow passage whence there was no escape, and experience a moment of panic fear. Yet it would be untrue to say he suffered. Mind and heart were drunk with passion, his footsteps guided by the daemonic power whose pastime it is to trample on human reason and dignity.

Tadzio and his sisters at length took a gondola. Aschenbach hid behind a portico or fountain while they embarked and directly they pushed off did the same. In a furtive whisper he told the boatman he would tip him well to follow at a little distance the other gondola, just rounding a corner, and fairly sickened at the man's quick, sly grasp and ready acceptance of the go-between's role.

Leaning back among soft, black cushions he swayed gently in the wake of the other black-snouted bark, to which the strength of his passion chained him. Sometimes it passed from his view, and then he was assailed by an anguish of unrest. But his guide appeared to have long practice in affairs like these; always, by dint of short cuts or deft manoeuvres, he contrived to overtake the coveted sight. The air was heavy and foul, the sun burnt down through a slate-coloured haze. Water slapped gurgling against wood and stone. The gondolier's cry, half warning, half salute, was answered with singular accord from far within the silence of the labyrinth. They passed little gardens high up the crumbling wall, hung with clustering white and purple flowers that sent down an odour of almonds. Moorish lattices showed shadowy in the gloom. The marble steps of a church descended into the canal, and on them a beggar squatted, displaying his misery to view, showing the whites of his eyes, holding out his hat for alms.

Farther on a dealer in antiquities cringed before his lair, inviting the passer-by to enter and be duped. Yes, this was Venice, this the fair frailty that fawned and that betrayed, half fairy-tale, half snare; the city in whose stagnating air the art of painting once put forth so lusty a growth, and where musicians were moved to accords so weirdly lulling and lascivious. Our adventurer felt his senses wooed by this voluptuousness of sight and sound, tasted his secret knowledge that the city sickened and hid its sickness for love of gain, and bent an ever more unbridled leer on the gondola that glided on before him.

It came at last to this – that his frenzy left him capacity for nothing else but to pursue his flame; to dream of him absent, to lavish, loverlike, endearing terms on his mere shadow. He was alone, he was a foreigner, he was sunk deep in this belated bliss of his – all which enabled him to pass unblushing through experiences well-nigh unbelievable. One night, returning late from Venice, he paused by his beloved's chamber door in the second storey, leaned his head against the panel, and remained there long, in utter drunkenness, powerless to tear himself away, blind to the danger of being caught in so mad an attitude.

And yet there were not wholly lacking moments when he paused and reflected, when in consternation he asked himself what path was this on which he had set his foot. Like most other men of parts and attainments, he had an aristocratic interest in his forbears, and when he achieved a success he liked to think he had gratified them, compelled their admiration and regard. He thought of them now, involved as he was in this illicit adventure, seized of these exotic excesses of feeling; thought of their stern self-command and decent manliness, and gave a melancholy smile. What would they have said? What, indeed, would they have said to his entire life, that varied to the point of degeneracy from theirs? This life in the bonds of art, had not he himself, in the days of his youth and in the very spirit of those bourgeois forefathers, pronounced mocking judgement upon it? And yet, at bottom, it had been so like their own! It had been a service, and he a soldier, like some of them; and art was war – a grilling, exhausting struggle that nowadays wore one out before one could grow old. It had been a life of self-conquest, a life against odds, dour, steadfast, abstinent; he had made it symbolical of the kind of over-strained heroism the time admired, and he was entitled to call it manly, even courageous. He wondered if such a life might not be somehow specially pleasing in the eyes of the god who had him in his power. For Eros had received most countenance among the most valiant nations – yes, were we not told that in their cities prowess made him flourish exceedingly? And many heroes of olden time had willingly borne his yoke, not counting any humiliation such as if it happened by the god's decree; vows, prostrations, self-abasements, these were no source of shame to the lover; rather they reaped him praise and honour.

Thus did the fond man's folly condition his thoughts; thus did he seek to hold his dignity upright in his own eyes. And all the while he kept doggedly on the traces of the disreputable secret the city kept hidden at its heart, just as he kept his own – and all that he learned fed his passion with vague, lawless hopes. He turned over newspapers at cafés, bent on finding a report on the progress of the disease; and in the German sheets, which had ceased to appear on the hotel table, he found a series of contradictory statements. The deaths, it was variously asserted, ran to twenty, to forty, to a hundred or more; yet in the next day's issue the existence of the pestilence was, if not roundly denied, reported as a matter of a few sporadic cases such as might be brought into a seaport town. After that the warnings would break out again, and the protests against the unscrupulous game the authorities were playing. No definite information was to be had.

And yet our solitary felt he had a sort of first claim on a

share in the unwholesome secret; he took a fantastic satisfaction in putting leading questions to such persons as were interested to conceal it, and forcing them to explicit untruths by way of denial. One day he attacked the manager, that small, soft-stepping man in the French frock-coat, who was moving about among the guests at luncheon, supervising the service and making himself socially agreeable. He paused at Aschenbach's table to exchange a greeting, and the guest put a question, with a negligent, casual air: 'Why in the world are they forever disinfecting the city of Venice?' 'A police regulation,' the adroit one replied; 'a precautionary measure, intended to protect the health of the public during this unseasonably warm and sultry weather.' 'Very praiseworthy of the police.' Aschenbach gravely responded. After a further exchange of meteorological commonplaces the manager passed on.

It happened that a band of street musicians came to perform in the hotel gardens that evening after dinner. They grouped themselves beneath an iron stanchion supporting an arc-light, two women and two men, and turned their faces, that shone white in the glare, up towards the guests who sat on the hotel terrace enjoying this popular entertainment along with their coffee and iced drinks. The hotel lift-boys, waiters, and office staff stood in the doorway and listened; the Russian family displayed the usual Russian absorption in their enjoyment – they had their chairs put down into the garden to be nearer the singers and sat there in a half-circle with gratitude painted on their features, the old serf in her turban erect behind their chairs.

These strolling players were adepts at mandolin, guitar, harmonica, even compassing a reedy violin. Vocal numbers alternated with instrumental, the younger woman, who had a high, shrill voice, joining in a love-duet with the sweetly falsettoing tenor. The actual head of the company, however, and incontestably its most gifted member, was the other man, who played the guitar. He was a sort of baritone buffo; with no voice to speak of, but possessed of a pantomimic gift and remarkable burlesque *élan*. Often he stepped out of the group and advanced towards the terrace, guitar in hand, and his audience rewarded his sallies with bursts of laughter. The Russians in their parterre seats were beside themselves with delight over this display of southern vivacity; their shouts and screams of applause encouraged him to bolder and bolder flights.

Aschenbach sat near the balustrade, a glass of pomegranate-juice and soda-water sparkling ruby-red before him, with which he now and then moistened his lips. His nerves drank in thirstily the unlovely sounds, the vulgar and sentimental tunes, for passion paralyses good taste and makes its victim accept with rapture what a man in his senses would either laugh at or turn from with disgust. Idly he sat and watched the antics of the buffoon with his face set in a fixed and painful smile, while inwardly his whole being was rigid with the intensity of the regard he bent on Tadzio, leaning over the railing six paces off.

He lounged there, in the white belted suit he sometimes wore at dinner, in all his innate, inevitable grace, with his left arm on the balustrade, his legs crossed, the right hand on the supporting hip; and looked down on the strolling singers with an expression that was hardly a smile, but rather a distant curiosity and polite toleration. Now and then he straightened himself and with a charming movement of both arms drew down his white blouse through his leather belt, throwing out his chest. And sometimes – Aschenbach saw it with triumph, with horror, and a sense that his reason was tottering – the lad would cast a glance, that might be slow and cautious, or might be sudden and swift, as though to take him by surprise, to the place where his lover sat. Aschenbach did not meet the glance. An ignoble caution made him keep his eyes in leash. For in the rear of the terrace sat Tadzio's mother and governess; and matters had gone so far that he feared to make himself conspicuous. Several times, on the beach, in the hotel lobby, on the Piazza, he had seen, with a stealing numbness, that they called Tadzio away from his neighbourhood. And his pride revolted at the affront, even while conscience told him it was deserved.

The performer below presently began a solo, with guitar accompaniment, a street song in several stanzas, just then the rage all over Italy. He delivered it in a striking and dramatic recitative, and his company joined in the refrain. He was a man of slight build, with a thin, undernourished face; his shabby felt hat rested on the back of his neck, a great mop of red hair sticking out in front; and he stood there on the gravel in advance of his troupe, in an impudent, swaggering posture, twanging the strings of his instrument and flinging a witty and rollicking recitative up to the terrace, while the veins on his forehead swelled with the violence of his effort. He was scarcely a Venetian type, belonging rather to the race of Neapolitan jesters, half bully, half comedian, brutal, blustering, an unpleasant customer, and entertaining to the last degree. The words of his song were trivial and silly, but on his lips, accompanied with gestures of head, hands, arms, and body, with leers and winks and the loose play of the tongue in the corner of his mouth, they took on meaning; an equivocal meaning, yet vaguely offensive. He wore a white sports shirt with a suit of ordinary clothes, and a strikingly large and naked-looking Adam's apple rose out of the open collar. From that pale, snub-nosed face it was hard to judge of his age; vice sat on it, it was furrowed with grimacing, and two deep wrinkles of defiance and self-will, almost of desperation, stood oddly between the red brows, above the grinning mobile mouth. But what more than all drew upon him the profound scrutiny of our solitary watcher was that this suspicious figure seemed to carry with it its own suspicious odour. For whenever the refrain occurred and the singer, with waving arms and antic gestures, passed in his grotesque march immediately beneath Aschenbach's seat, a strong smell of carbolic was wafted up to the terrace.

After the song he began to take up money, beginning with the Russian family, who gave liberally, and then mounting the steps to the terrace. But here he became as cringing as he had before been forward. He glided between the tables, bowing and scraping, showing his strong white teeth in a servile smile, though the two deep furrows on the brow were still very marked. His audience looked at the strange creature as he went about collecting his livelihood, and their curiosity was not unmixed with disfavour. They tossed coins with their finger-tips into his hat and took care not to touch it. Let the enjoyment be never so great, a sort of embarrassment always comes when the comedian oversteps the physical distance between himself and respectable people. This man felt it and sought to make his peace by fawning. He came along the railing to Aschenbach, and with him came that smell no one else seemed to notice.

'Listen!' said the solitary, in a low voice, almost mechanically; 'they are disinfecting Venice – why?' The mountebank answered hoarsely: 'Because of the police. Orders, signore. On account of the heat and the sirocco. The sirocco is oppressive. Not good for the health.' He spoke as though surprised that anyone could ask, and with the flat of his hand he demonstrated how oppressive the sirocco was. 'So there is no plague in Venice?' Aschenbach asked the question between his teeth, very low. The man's expressive face fell, he put on a look of comical innocence. 'A plague? What sort of plague? Is the sirocco a plague? Or perhaps our police are a plague! You are making fun of us, signore! A plague! Why should there be? The police make regulations on account of the heat and the weather. . . .' He gestured. 'Quite,' said Aschenbach, once more, soft and low; and dropping an unduly large coin into the man's hat dismissed him with a sign. He bowed very low and left. But he had not reached the steps when two of the hotel servants flung themselves on him and began to whisper, their faces close to his. He shrugged, seemed to be giving assurances, to be swearing he had said nothing. It was not hard to guess the import of his words. They let him go at last and he went back into the garden, where he conferred briefly with his troupe and then stepped forward for a farewell song.

It was one Aschenbach had never to his knowledge heard before, a rowdy air, with words in impossible dialect. It had a laughing-refrain in which the other three artists joined at the top of their lungs. The refrain had neither words nor accompaniment, it was nothing but rhythmical, modulated, natural laughter, which the soloist in particular knew how to render with most deceptive realism. Now that he was farther off his audience, his self-assurance had come back, and this laughter of his rang with a mocking note. He would be overtaken, before he reached the end of the last line of each stanza; he would catch his breath, lay his hand over his mouth, his voice would quaver and his shoulders shake, he would lose power to contain himself longer. Just at the right moment each time, it came whooping, bawling, crashing out of him, with a verisimilitude that never failed to set his audience off in profuse and unpremeditated mirth that seemed to add gusto to his own. He bent his knees, he clapped his thigh, he held his sides, he looked ripe for bursting. He no longer laughed, but yelled, pointing his finger at the company there above as though there could be in all the world nothing so comic as they; until at last they laughed in hotel, terrace, and garden, down to the waiters, lift-boys, and servants – laughed as though possessed.

Aschenbach could no longer rest in his chair, he sat poised for flight. But the combined effect of the laughing, the hospital odour in his nostrils, and the nearness of the beloved was to hold him in a spell; he felt unable to stir. Under cover of the general commotion he looked across at Tadzio and saw that the lovely boy returned his gaze with a seriousness that seemed the copy of his own; the general hilarity, it seemed to say, had no power over him, he kept aloof. The grey-haired man was overpowered, disarmed by this docile, childlike deference; with difficulty he refrained from hiding his face in his hands. Tadzio's habit, too, of drawing himself up and taking a deep sighing breath struck him as being due to an oppression of the chest. 'He is sickly, he will never live to grow up,' he thought once again, with that dispassionate vision to which his madness of desire sometimes so strangely gave way. And compassion struggled with the reckless exultation of his heart.

The players, meanwhile, had finished and gone; their leader bowing and scraping, kissing his hands and adorning his leave-taking with antics that grew madder with the applause they evoked. After all the others were outside, he pretended to run backwards full tilt against a lamp-post and slunk to the gate apparently doubled over with pain. But there he threw off his buffoon's mask, stood erect, with an elastic straightening of his whole figure, ran out his tongue impudently at the guests on the terrace, and vanished in the night. The company dispersed. Tadzio had long since left the balustrade. But he, the lonely man, sat for long, to the waiters' great annoyance, before the dregs of pomegranate-juice in his glass. Time passed, the night went on. Long ago, in his parental home, he had watched the sand filter through an hour-glass – he could still see, as though it stood before him, the fragile, pregnant little toy. Soundless and fine the rust-red streamlet ran through the narrow neck and made, as it declined in the upper cavity, an exquisite little vortex.

The very next afternoon the solitary took another step in pursuit of his fixed policy of baiting the outer world. This time he had all possible success. He went, that is, into the English travel bureau in the Piazza, changed some money at the desk, and posing as the suspicious foreigner, put his fateful question. The clerk was a tweed-clad young Britisher, with his eyes set close together, his hair parted in the middle, and radiating that steady reliability which makes his like so strange a phenomenon in the *gamin*, agile-witted south. He began: 'No ground for alarm, sir. A mere formality. Quite regular in view of the unhealthy climatic conditions.' But then, looking up, he chanced to meet with his own blue eyes the stranger's weary, melancholy gaze, fixed on his face. The Englishman coloured. He continued in a lower voice, rather confused: 'At least, that is the official explanation, which they see fit to stick to. I may tell you there's a bit more to it than that.' And then, in his good, straightforward way, he told the truth.

For the past several years Asiatic cholera had shown a strong tendency to spread. Its source was the hot, moist swamps of the delta of the Ganges, where it bred in the mephitic air of that primeval island-jungle, among whose bamboo thickets the tiger crouches, where life of every sort flourishes in rankest abundance, and only man avoids the spot. Thence the pestilence had spread throughout Hindustan, ranging with great violence; moved eastwards to China, westward to Afghanistan and Persia; following the great caravan routes, it brought terror to Astrakhan, terror to Moscow. Even while Europe trembled lest the spectre be seen striding westward across country, it was carried by sea from Syrian ports and appeared simultaneously at several points on the Mediterranean littoral; raised its head in Toulon and Malaga, Palermo and Naples, and soon got a firm hold in Calabria and Apulia. Northern Italy had been spared – so far. But in May the horrible vibrios were found on the same day in two bodies: the emaciated, blackened corpses of a bargee and a woman who kept a greengrocer's shop. Both cases were hushed up. But in a week there were ten more – twenty, thirty in different quarters of the town. An Austrian provincial, having come to Venice on a few days' pleasure trip, went home and died with all the symptoms of the plague. Thus was explained the fact that the

German-language papers were the first to print the news of the Venetian outbreak. The Venetian authorities published in reply a statement to the effect that the state of the city's health had never been better; at the same time instituting the most necessary precautions. But by that time the food supplies – milk, meat, or vegetables – had probably been contaminated, for death unseen and unacknowledged was devouring and laying waste in the narrow streets, while a brooding, unseasonable heat warmed the waters of the canals and encouraged the spread of the pestilence. Yes, the disease seemed to flourish and wax strong, to redouble its generative powers. Recoveries were rare. Eighty out of every hundred died, and horribly, for the onslaught was of the extremest violence, and not infrequently of the 'dry' type, the most malignant form of the contagion. In this form the victim's body loses power to expel the water secreted by the blood-vessels, it shrivels up, he passes with hoarse cries from convulsion to convulsion, his blood grows thick like pitch and he suffocates in a few hours. He is fortunate indeed, if, as sometimes happens, the disease, after a slight *malaise*, takes the form of a profound unconsciousness, from which the sufferer seldom or never rouses. By the beginning of June the quarantine buildings of the *ospedale civico* had quietly filled up, the two orphan asylums were entirely occupied, and there was a hideously brisk traffic between the *Nuovo Fundamento* and the island of San Michele, where the cemetery was. But the city was not swayed by high-minded motives or regard for international agreements. The authorities were more actuated by fear of being out of pocket, by regard for the new exhibition of paintings just opened in the Public Gardens, or by apprehension of the large losses the hotels and the shops that catered to foreigners would suffer in case of panic and blockade. And the fears of the people supported the persistent official policy of silence and denial. The city's first medical officer, an honest and competent man, had indignantly resigned his office and been privily replaced by a more compliant person. The fact was known; and this corruption in high places played its part, together with the suspense as to where the walking terror might strike next, to demoralize the baser elements in the city and encourage those antisocial forces which shun the light of day. There was intemperance, indecency, increase of crime. Evenings one saw many drunken people, which was unusual. Gangs of men in surly mood made the streets unsafe, theft and assault were said to be frequent, even murder; for in two cases persons supposedly victims of the plague were proved to have been poisoned by their own families. And professional vice was rampant, displaying excesses heretofore unknown and only at home much farther south and in the east.

Such was the substance of the Englishman's tale. 'You would do well,' he concluded, 'to leave to-day instead of to-morrow. The blockade cannot be more than a few days off.'

'Thank you,' said Aschenbach, and left the office.

The Piazza lay in sweltering sunshine. Innocent foreigners sat before the cafés or stood in front of the cathedral, the centre of clouds of doves that, with fluttering wings, tried to shoulder each other away and pick the kernels of maize from the extended hand. Aschenbach strode up and down the spacious flags, feverishly excited, triumphant in possession of the truth at last, but with a sickening taste in his mouth and a fantastic horror at his heart. One decent, expiatory course lay open to him; he considered it. To-night, after dinner, he might approach the lady of the pearls and address her in words which he precisely formulated in his mind: 'Madame, will you permit an entire stranger to serve you with a word of advice and warning which self-interest prevents others from uttering? Go away. Leave here at once, without delay, with Tadzio and your daughters. Venice is in the grip of pestilence.' Then might he lay his hand in farewell upon the head of that instrument of a mocking deity; and thereafter himself flee the accursed morass. But he knew that he was far indeed from any

serious desire to take such a step. It would restore him, would
give him back himself once more; but he who is beside himself revolts at the idea of self-possession. There crossed his
mind the vision of a white building with inscriptions on it,
glittering in the sinking sun – he recalled how his mind had
dreamed away into their transparent mysticism; recalled the
strange pilgrim apparition that had wakened in the ageing man
a lust for strange countries and fresh sights. And these
memories again brought in their train the thought of returning home, returning to reason, self-mastery, an ordered
existence, to the old life of effort. Alas! the bare thought
made him wince with a revulsion that was like physical
nausea. 'It must be kept quiet,' he whispered fiercely. 'I will
not speak!' The knowledge that he shared the city's secret, the
city's guilt – it put him beside himself, intoxicated him as a
small quantity of wine will a man suffering from brain-fag.
His thoughts dwelt upon the image of the desolate and calami-
tous city, and he was giddy with fugitive, mad, unreasoning
hopes and visions of a monstrous sweetness. That tender
sentiment he had a moment ago evoked, what was it compared with such images as these? His art, his moral sense, what
were they in the balance beside the boons that chaos might
confer? He kept silence, he stopped on.

That night he had a fearful dream – if dream be the right
word for a mental and physical experience which did indeed
befall him in deep sleep, as a thing quite apart and real to his
senses, yet without his seeing himself as present in it. Rather
its theatre seemed to be his own soul, and the events burst in
from outside, violently overcoming the profound resistance
of his spirit; passed him through and left him, left the whole
cultural structure of a life-time trampled on, ravaged, and
destroyed.

The beginning was fear; fear and desire, with a shuddering
curiosity. Night reigned, and his senses were on the alert; he
heard loud, confused noises from far away, clamour and

hubbub. There was a rattling, a crashing, a low dull thunder;
shrill halloos and a kind of howl with a long-drawn *u*-sound
at the end. And with all these, dominating them all, flute-
notes of the cruellest sweetness, deep and cooing, keeping
shamelessly on until the listener felt his very entrails bewitched. He heard a voice, naming, though darkly, that which
was to come: 'The stranger god!' A glow lighted up the
surrounding mist and by it he recognized a mountain scene
like that about his country home. From the wooded heights,
from among the tree-trunks and crumbling moss-covered
rocks, a troop came tumbling and raging down, a whirling
rout of men and animals, and overflowed the hillside with
flames and human forms, with clamour and the reeling dance.
The females stumbled over the long, hairy pelts that dangled
from their girdles; with heads flung back they uttered loud
hoarse cries and shook their tambourines high in air; bran-
dished naked daggers or torches vomiting trails of sparks.
They shrieked, holding their breasts in both hands; coiling
snakes with quivering tongues they clutched about their
waists. Horned and hairy males, girt about the loins with
hides, drooped heads and lifted arms and thighs in unison, as
they beat on brazen vessels that gave out droning thunder,
or thumped madly on drums. There were troops of beardless
youths armed with garlanded staves; these ran after goats and
thrust their staves against the creatures' flanks, then clung to
the plunging horns and let themselves be borne off with
triumphant shouts. And one and all the mad rout yelled that
cry, composed of soft consonants with a long-drawn *u*-sound
at the end, so sweet and wild it was together, and like nothing
ever heard before! It would ring through the air like the
bellow of a challenging stag, and be given back many-
tongued; or they would use it to goad each other on to dance
with wild excess of tossing limbs – they never let it die. But
the deep, beguiling notes of the flute wove in and out and
over all. Beguiling too it was to him who struggled in the grip

of these sights and sounds, shamelessly awaiting the coming
feast and the uttermost surrender. He trembled, he shrank, his
will was steadfast to preserve and uphold his own god against
this stranger who was sworn enemy to dignity and self-control. But the mountain wall took up the noise and howling
and gave it back manifold; it rose high, swelled to a madness that carried him away. His senses reeled in the steam of
panting bodies, the acrid stench from the goats, the odour as
of stagnant waters – and another, too familiar smell – of
wounds, uncleanness, and disease. His heart throbbed to the
drums, his brain reeled, a blind rage seized him, a whirling
lust, he craved with all his soul to join the ring that formed
about the obscene symbol of the godhead, which they were
unveiling and elevating, monstrous and wooden, while from
full throats they yelled their rallying-cry. Foam dripped from
their lips, they drove each other on with lewd gesturings and
beckoning hands. They laughed, they howled, they thrust
their pointed staves into each other's flesh and licked the blood
as it ran down. But now the dreamer was in them and of them,
the stranger god was his own. Yes, it was he who was flinging
himself upon the animals, who bit and tore and swallowed
smoking gobbets of flesh – while on the trampled moss there
now began the rites in honour of the god, an orgy of promis-
cuous embraces – and in his very soul he tasted the bestial
degradation of his fall.

The unhappy man woke from this dream shattered, un-
hinged, powerless in the demon's grip. He no longer avoided
men's eyes nor cared whether he exposed himself to suspicion.
And anyhow, people were leaving; many of the bathing-
cabins stood empty, there were many vacant places in the
dining-room, scarcely any foreigners were seen in the streets.
The truth seemed to have leaked out; despite all efforts to the
contrary, panic was in the air. But the lady of the pearls
stopped on with her family; whether because the rumours
had not reached her or because she was too proud and fearless

to heed them. Tadzio remained; and it seemed at times to Aschenbach, in his obsessed state, that death and fear together might clear the island of all other souls and leave him there alone with him he coveted. In the long mornings on the beach his heavy gaze would rest, a fixed and reckless stare, upon the lad; towards nightfall, lost to shame, he would follow him through the city's narrow streets where horrid death stalked too, and at such time it seemed to him as though the moral law were fallen in ruins and only the monstrous and perverse held out a hope.

Like any lover, he desired to please; suffered agonies at the thought of failure, and brightened his dress with smart ties and handkerchiefs and other youthful touches. He added jewellery and perfumes and spent hours each day over his toilette, appearing at dinner elaborately arrayed and tensely excited. The presence of the youthful beauty that had bewitched him filled him with disgust of his own ageing body; the sight of his own sharp features and grey hair plunged him in hopeless mortification; he made desperate efforts to recover the appearance and freshness of his youth and began paying frequent visits to the hotel barber. Enveloped in the white sheet, beneath the hands of that garrulous personage, he would lean back in the chair and look at himself in the glass with misgiving.

'Grey,' he said, with a grimace.

'Slightly,' answered the man. 'Entirely due to neglect, to a lack of regard for appearances. Very natural, of course, in men of affairs, but, after all, not very sensible, for it is just such people who ought to be above vulgar prejudice in matters like these. Some folk have very strict ideas about the use of cosmetics; but they never extend them to the teeth, as they logically should. And very disgusted other people would be if they did. No, we are all as old as we feel, but no older, and grey hair can misrepresent a man worse than dyed. You, for instance, signore, have a right to your natural colour. Surely you will permit me to restore what belongs to you?'

'How?' asked Aschenbach.

For answer the oily one washed his client's hair in two waters, one clear and one dark, and lo, it was as black as in the days of his youth. He waved it with the tongs in wide, flat undulations, and stepped back to admire the effect.

'Now if we were just to freshen up the skin a little,' he said. And with that he went on from one thing to another, his enthusiasm waxing with each new idea. Aschenbach sat there comfortably; he was incapable of objecting to the process – rather as it went forward it roused his hopes. He watched it in the mirror and saw his eyebrows grow more even and arching, the eyes gain in size and brilliance, by dint of a little application below the lids. A delicate carmine glowed on his cheeks where the skin had been so brown and leathery. The dry, anaemic lips grew full, they turned the colour of ripe strawberries, the lines round eyes and mouth were treated with a facial cream and gave place to youthful bloom. It was a young man who looked back at him from the glass – Aschenbach's heart leaped at the sight. The artist in cosmetic at last professed himself satisfied; after the manner of such people, he thanked his client profusely for what he had done himself. 'The merest trifle, the merest, signore,' he said as he added the final touches. 'Now the signore can fall in love as soon as he likes.' Aschenbach went off as in a dream, dazed between joy and fear, in his red neck-tie and broad straw hat with its gay striped band.

A lukewarm storm-wind had come up. It rained a little now and then, the air was heavy and turbid and smelt of decay. Aschenbach, with fevered cheeks beneath the rouge, seemed to hear rushing and flapping sounds in his ears, as though storm-spirits were abroad – unhallowed ocean harpies who follow those devoted to destruction, snatch away and defile their viands. For the heat took away his appetite and thus he was haunted with the idea that his food was infected.

One afternoon he pursued his charmer deep into the stricken

city's huddled heart. The labyrinthine little streets, squares,
canals, and bridges, each one so like the next, at length quite
made him lose his bearings. He did not even know the points
of the compass; all his care was not to lose sight of the figure
after which his eyes thirsted. He slunk under walls, he lurked
behind buildings or people's backs; and the sustained tension
of his senses and emotions exhausted him more and more,
though for a long time he was unconscious of fatigue. Tadzio
walked behind the others, he let them pass ahead in the narrow
alleys, and as he sauntered slowly after, he would turn his
head and assure himself with a glance of his strange, twilit
grey eyes that his lover was still following. He saw him – and
he did not betray him. The knowledge enraptured Aschenbach. Lured by those eyes, led on the leading-string of his own
passion and folly, utterly lovesick, he stole upon the footsteps of his unseemly hope – and at the end found himself
cheated. The Polish family crossed a small vaulted bridge, the
height of whose archway hid them from his sight, and when
he climbed it himself they were nowhere to be seen. He
hunted in three directions – straight ahead and on both sides
of the narrow, dirty quay – in vain. Worn quite out and un-
nerved, he had to give over the search.

His head burned, his body was wet with clammy sweat, he
was plagued by intolerable thirst. He looked about for refresh-
ment, of whatever sort, and found a little fruit-shop where he
bought some strawberries. They were overripe and soft; he
ate them as he went. The street he was on opened out into a
little square, one of those charmed, forsaken spots he liked;
he recognized it as the very one where he had sat weeks ago
and conceived his abortive plan of flight. He sank down on the
steps of the well and leaned his head against its stone rim. It
was quiet here. Grass grew between the stones and rubbish
lay about. Tall, weather-beaten houses bordered the square,
one of them rather palatial, with vaulted windows, gaping
now, and little lion balconies. In the ground floor of another

was an apothecary's shop. A waft of carbolic acid was borne
on a warm gust of wind.

There he sat, the master: this was he who had found a way
to reconcile art and honours; who had written *The Abject*, and
in a style of classic purity renounced bohemianism and all its
works, all sympathy with the abyss and the troubled depths of
the outcast human soul. This was he who had put knowledge
underfoot to climb so high; who had outgrown the ironic
pose and adjusted himself to the burdens and obligations of
fame; whose renown had been officially recognized and his
name ennobled, whose style was set for a model in the schools.
There he sat. His eyelids were closed, there was only a swift,
sidelong glint of the eyeballs now and again, something
between a question and a leer; while the rouged and flabby
mouth uttered single words of the sentences shaped in his dis-
ordered brain by the fantastic logic that governs our dreams.

'For mark you, Phaedrus, beauty alone is both divine and
visible; and so it is the sense's way, the artist's way, little
Phaedrus, to the spirit. But, now tell me, my dear boy, do you
believe that such a man can ever attain wisdom and true
manly worth, for whom the path to the spirit must lead
through the senses? Or do you rather think – for I leave the
point to you – that it is a path of perilous sweetness, a way of
transgression, and must surely lead him who walks in it
astray? For you know that we poets cannot walk the way of
beauty without Eros as our companion and guide. We may
be heroic after our fashion, disciplined warriors of our craft,
yet are we all like women, for we exult in passion, and love
is still our desire – our craving and our shame. And from this
you will perceive that we poets can be neither wise nor worthy
citizens. We must needs be wanton, must needs rove at large
in the realm of feeling. Our magisterial style is all folly and
pretence, our honourable repute a farce, the crowd's belief
in us is merely laughable. And to teach youth, or the populace, by means of art is a dangerous practice and ought to be

forbidden. For what good can an artist be as a teacher, when from his birth up he is headed direct for the pit? We may want to shun it and attain to honour in the world; but however we turn, it draws us still. So, then, since knowledge might destroy us, we will have none of it. For knowledge, Phaedrus, does not make him who possesses it dignified or austere. Knowledge is all-knowing, understanding, forgiving; it takes up no position, sets no store by form. It has compassion with the abyss – it *is* the abyss. So we reject it, firmly, and henceforward our concern shall be with beauty only. And by beauty we mean simplicity, largeness, and renewed severity of discipline; we mean a return to detachment and to form. But detachment, Phaedrus, and preoccupation with form lead to intoxication and desire, they may lead the noblest among us to frightful emotional excesses, which his own stern cult of the beautiful would make him the first to condemn. So they too, they too, lead to the bottomless pit. Yes, they lead us thither, I say, us who are poets – who by our natures are prone not to excellence but to excess. And now, Phaedrus, I will go. Remain here; and only when you can no longer see me, then do you depart also.'

A few days later, Gustave Aschenbach left his hotel rather later than usual in the morning. He was not feeling well and had to struggle against spells of giddiness only half physical in their nature, accompanied by a swiftly mounting dread, a sense of futility and hopelessness – but whether this referred to himself or to the outer world he could not tell. In the lobby he saw a quantity of luggage lying strapped and ready; asked the porter whose it was, and received in answer the name he already knew he should hear – that of the Polish family. The expression of his ravaged features did not change; he only gave that quick lift of the head with which we sometimes receive the uninteresting answer to a casual query. But he put another: 'When?' 'After luncheon,' the man replied. He nodded, and went down to the beach.

It was an unfriendly scene. Little crisping shivers ran all across the wide stretch of shallow water between the shore and the first sand-bank. The whole beach, once so full of colour and life, looked now autumnal, out of season; it was nearly deserted and not even very clean. A camera on a tripod stood at the edge of the water, apparently abandoned; its black cloth snapped in the freshening wind.

Tadzio was there, in front of his cabin, with the three or four playfellows still left him. Aschenbach set up his chair some half-way between the cabins and the water, spread a rug over his knees, and sat looking on. The game this time was unsupervised, the elders being probably busy with the packing, and it looked rather lawless and out-of-hand. Jaschiu, the sturdy lad in the belted suit, with the black, brilliantined hair, became angry at a handful of sand thrown in his eyes; he challenged Tadzio to a fight, which quickly ended in the downfall of the weaker. And perhaps the coarser nature saw here a chance to avenge himself at last, by one cruel act, for his long weeks of subserviency: the victor would not let the vanquished get up, but remained kneeling on Tadzio's back, pressing Tadzio's face into the sand – for so long a time that it seemed the exhausted lad might even suffocate. He made spasmodic efforts to shake the other off, lay still and then began a feeble twitching. Just as Aschenbach was about to spring indignantly to the rescue, Jaschiu let his victim go. Tadzio, very pale, half sat up, and remained so, leaning on one arm, for several minutes, with darkening eyes and rumpled hair. Then he rose and walked slowly away. The others called him, at first gaily, then imploringly; he would not hear. Jaschiu was evidently overtaken by swift remorse; he followed his friend and tried to make his peace, but Tadzio motioned him back with a jerk of one shoulder and went down to the water's edge. He was barefoot and wore his striped linen suit with the red breast-knot.

There he stayed a little, with bent head, tracing figures in the wet sand with one toe; then stepped into the shallow water, which at its deepest did not wet his knees; waded idly through it and reached the sand-bar. Now he paused again with his face turned seaward; and next began to move slowly leftwards along the narrow strip of sand the sea left bare. He paced there, divided by an expanse of water from the shore, from his mates by his moody pride; a remote and isolated figure with floating locks, out there in sea and wind, against the misty inane. Once more he paused to look: with a sudden recollection, or by an impulse, he turned from the waist up, in an exquisite movement, one hand resting on his hip, and looked over his shoulder at the shore. The watcher sat just as he had sat that time in the lobby of the hotel when first the twilit grey eyes had met his own. He rested his head against the chair-back and followed the movements of the figure out there, then lifted it, as it were in answer to Tadzio's gaze. It sank on his breast, the eyes looked out beneath their lids, while his whole face took on the relaxed and brooding expression of deep slumber. It seemed to him the pale and lovely Summoner out there smiled at him and beckoned; as though with the hand he lifted from his hip, he pointed outward as he hovered on before into an immensity of richest expectation.

Some minutes passed before anyone hastened to the aid of the elderly man sitting there collapsed in his chair. They bore him to his room. And before nightfall a shocked and respectful world received the news of his decease.

1911

Thomas Mann was born in 1875, in the North German town of Lübeck. His father was a member of the local Hanseatic bourgeoisie, a merchant by profession and a senator on the city council, and his mother was of South American descent, part Portuguese and part Creole. His elder brother was the novelist Heinrich Mann. His early childhood and school years were spent in Lübeck, and at the age of nineteen he went to Munich where he joined an insurance company. In his free time he studied literature and eventually attended the University of Munich. After a year in Rome he returned to Germany. He married Katja Pringsheim in 1905 and they had six children. His earlier major works include *Buddenbrooks* (1901), *Death in Venice* (1911), *Royal Highness* (1916) and *The Magic Mountain* (1924). During the 1920s Mann supported the Weimar Republic on his many lecture tours in Germany and abroad, and in 1929 was awarded the Nobel Prize for Literature. With Hitler's rise to power, Mann decided to live in Switzerland and publicly dissociated himself from the National Socialist regime. He was deprived of his German citizenship in 1936. During this period he wrote the biblical tetralogy *Joseph and his Brothers*. He was visiting professor to Princeton in 1938 and wrote *Lotte in Weimar*, before settling in California where he was in close touch with other distinguished German emigrant writers and artists. He wrote *Doctor Faustus* and *The Holy Sinner*. In 1944 he became a citizen of the United States. He revisited Germany in 1949 and in 1952 returned to Switzerland where *The Black Swan* (1954) and *Confessions of Felix Krull, Confidence Man* (1955) were written. He died in 1955.

Thomas Mann has been described as the greatest German writer of this century. In the words of one critic he wrested 'a stupendous and wonderful body of achievement from a seemingly exhausted and crumbling art form, remaking it from step to step as he went along. He has proved that it is still possible to write great, profoundly original and relevant novels, without falling either into academic sterility or [into] obscurity and unreadability.'